TRUTH

TRUTH

AZOPHI ACADEMY™ BOOK FOUR

TR CAMERON   MICHAEL ANDERLE   MARTHA CARR

DISRUPTIVE IMAGINATION

Copyright © LMBPN Publishing
Cover by Cover by Fantasy Book Design
Cover copyright © LMBPN Publishing
A Michael Anderle Production

LMBPN Publishing
PMB 196, 2540 South Maryland Pkwy
Las Vegas, NV 89109

First US edition, October, 2020
ebook ISBN: 978-1-64971-278-3
Print ISBN: 978-1-64971-279-0

For those who seek wonder around every corner and in each turning page. And, as always, for Dylan and Laurel.

— T.R. Cameron

Thanks to our JIT Readers

Kelly O'Donnell
Dave Hicks
Deb Mader
James Caplan
Kerry Mortimer
Diane L. Smith
Veronica Stephan-Miller
Jeff Goode
Larry Omans

Editor

SkyHunter Editing Team

CHAPTER ONE

Special Forces Captain Jackson Reese stepped off the moon shuttle at the spaceport in Edinburgh, Scotland, Earth. He'd been off-planet chasing down a lead that had failed to pan out to anything useful. It was the fourth or fifth such strand he'd plucked that had led exactly nowhere. He was looking forward to getting back to the Academy, and hopefully convincing Juno that a third date would be something she'd enjoy. It wouldn't overcome his frustration at the lack of progress on his main mission, but it would be far more fun than the endless searching had proven to be. *Somewhere out there, I'm going to find the clue that brings down Arlox. But I have to admit, the key to that particular lock is pretty damn well hidden.*

Athena, the artificial intelligence that resided inside his brain and was steadily spreading her tendrils throughout his body, replied, "Seems unlikely. Maybe you should ask someone smarter than you for help."

He scowled as he grabbed his bag from the conveyor

belt that connected the tarmac with the terminal. *Shut up, you. No comments from the peanut gallery.*

"What does that mean? I can find no record of it in my memory."

He snorted. *I guess the all-knowing AI isn't actually all-knowing, huh?*

Athena made a sound like a growl. "Accessing network. Searching." An instant later, she continued, "A reference to theater, and also used in baseball. I imagine that's another thing you would be terrible at."

He chuckled, then smiled innocently at the people who stared at him strangely for doing so. As her personality had become more developed, restraining his external reactions to her had become more difficult. *I was pretty good if you want to know the truth. Why, one time...*

Athena interrupted, "Move diagonally to your left, same pace, now." Jax had learned not to argue when she gave him a direct command and shifted position in the indicated direction without altering his stride. "At least three people in our vicinity decisively reacted to your movement. I believe we are being watched."

Send out an alert to everybody, now.

"On it."

They'd all known it was a matter of time before Arlox and his Intelligence Division flunkies came after one or more of them. They'd created a preset communication routine that would warn Professor Maarsen, Major Anika Stephenson on board the *Cronus*, plus Juno, the members of his Special Forces team, and the people he teamed with on Academy missions. *What are they doing?*

"Two of them are trailing, maintaining a steady

distance from us. Ahead and to the right, one is in position to block our exit or follow if we leave that way."

Dammit. Guess the fastest path to the maglev is out. Let's try the other exit, and see if we can lead them away and circle back.

"Down." Athena's voice was almost a screech, and Jax threw himself forward into a roll. The soft *thwack* of bullets striking the bag slung over his shoulder eliminated all doubt about the intent of those following them. *Hunter team. Has to be. That means there's at least one more, and maybe two to four in reserve.* He surged to his feet and ran, dodging and weaving toward the far doors. After a few steps, his bag fell to the floor as its damaged strap snapped. He ignored it and kept moving.

As he approached the exit, the fourth member of the opposition came into view. He wore a tan suit with a black tie over a white shirt, and an innocuous expression graced his face. Dark sunglasses hid his eyes, and the man's brown hair and average build would have ensured his anonymity almost anywhere. However, the large pistol coming up in his right hand was an unmistakable sign of his difference from those around him. His neutral visage didn't change as he lined up the weapon and pulled the trigger. Jax dropped and rolled, and the bullets that would've smashed into his head passed over it instead.

This is insane. It's a public place, with civilian authorities. They've always tried to operate in secret. Why would they choose to do it differently here? But figuring out the answer to that contradiction wasn't nearly as important right now as finding a way out of the trap he'd walked into. Athena warned, "They're closing in from all directions. You need to get out of here."

Tell me something I don't know. Give me a jolt. Jax scrambled to his right and accelerated into a run toward the obviously guarded exit closest to the maglev station. Energy flooded through his body as Athena pumped him with adrenaline and endorphins to make him faster and stronger than normal. It seemed like the world took on a sharpness when it hit, everything suddenly rendered in substantially greater clarity. He ran a serpentine path through the crowd, lacking any other options to avoid getting shot, and was pleased when the enemy agent didn't simply mow down the innocents filling the terminal. He'd counted on at least that much discretion from them. *Now if only a little help would arrive, I'd be set.*

No sooner had he acknowledged the thought than a pair of security officers showed up, shouting and pointing their guns at the agent who had last fired at him, off to his left. That man shifted his aim and dropped both guards before they could fire a shot. *Dammit. They're serious about taking me out regardless of the consequences to anyone above the level of an innocent bystander. Maybe not even them.*

Weapons weren't permitted on the shuttle he'd taken down, so he wasn't carrying a pistol. He was far from defenseless, however. He poured on all his enhanced speed and charged the man between him and the exit in a flurry of swaying, ducking, and dodging. His opponent sighted carefully and squeezed the trigger several times. A round caught Jax in his right arm and triggered an immediate burning that became an angry throbbing, which washed through the limb like a wave of fire extending to his fingertips. He growled under his breath, "Hell and damnation, why do they always shoot the real arm?"

Jax closed the distance before the agent could get off another shot and channeled his momentum into a punch. He used his unwounded left arm: the one that had been shredded beyond repair by an explosion on a distant planet, and had been replaced by a prosthetic that was faster, stronger, and far more deadly. It jabbed out in a simple, direct strike at his foe's sternum, delivering the entire power of his velocity and the adrenaline-boosted speed that his passenger had given him. It crushed the bones in the man's chest and knocked him flying backward. He fell, gasping and retching, and Jax paused for a moment to snag his dropped pistol before barreling out through the doors.

Athena shouted, "Right." Jax dodged, and a bullet slammed into the wall beside his head. *Didn't hear the shot. Must be a sniper.* He ran in a bobbing crouch that traded speed for avoiding offering a clear target to the gunman. *Gonna need you to step up, Athena.*

"I've got you," she replied. From off to his left came the sound of a distant scream, like it might've come from the roof of one of the low buildings nearby. No further shots hounded him as he pounded toward the maglev station.

What did you do?

"Hacked a traffic drone. Knocked him off the building with it."

He laughed. "Nice." He only realized he'd spoken aloud when he got even stranger looks from the people he was running past. "Fine, whatever, who cares if everyone thinks I'm crazy. What's the status of the others?"

Athena replied, "I received the expected acknowledgments, but nothing more. As the protocol requires," she reminded him.

"Yeah, yeah," he grumbled.

"I'm sure Juno is safe."

A bullet slammed into his shoulder, and Jax cursed as it threw him off balance. He stumbled and fell, and scraped his hands on the sidewalk, but pushed himself into a roll and came up weaving. "What the hell?"

"Long-distance shot. Pistol from a block away. Quit whining."

"You suck." If he needed to, he could ask the AI to turn off his pain receptors, but prior experience had shown that choice tended to lead only to greater injury. It was very much a last resort. Fortunately, the moving staircase that led up to the maglev station was directly ahead. *Once I get on board, I'll be safe.* The trains were frequent enough that he figured he'd be able to snag one before they could catch up to him. *Check the cameras in the maglev station. Anything I need to worry about?*

"Accessing." He stepped onto the moving stairs and did his best to blend in while the crowded escalator conveyed them up the multiple stories to the platform and tracks. Athena reported, "No apparent enemies in the station, or at least none resembling those who were at the spaceport."

Good. What about the ones behind us?

"Half a block away and closing."

Jax pushed his way forward, figuring he would cross the last quarter of the ascent faster to gain some distance on those pursuing him. It came as a shock when one of the people he'd taken for a college student or something similar, dressed in a concert T-shirt and carrying a backpack festooned with band name patches on it, suddenly smashed an elbow back at his face. If the attack had come from the left side, his quickened limb might've been able to catch it despite his complete surprise. But it came from his right, and the elbow drove into his nose and broke it with a crunch that echoed in his ears.

Tears flowed immediately and obscured his vision as he ducked and twisted and punched at his opponent's spine. His fist connected, and the man screamed. Another person right in front of Jax had turned and put his hands on the banisters to launch himself in a flying kick at Jax's throat. There was nowhere to run and no time to fully dodge the blow. Instead, he hurled himself forward, caught the kick on crossed forearms, and narrowly avoided getting knocked off balance and back down the escalator.

The man in front of him fell onto his back, and Jax vaulted over him to land on the maglev station's main floor. He slipped on the well-polished tile, then righted himself and pelted toward the trains, slowing only to swipe his wrist comm over the ticket sensor to pay for his ride. The crack of a gun from behind him caused him to crouch reflexively. He slid to a stop and yanked the agent's pistol from the pocket he'd shoved it into. He aimed and pulled the trigger, but nothing happened. He spun and ran again. *Dammit, Athena, why didn't you override the biometrics?*

"I did. It must be another transponder backup." They'd faced intelligence agents before who had physical transponders that acted as a second level of security on their weapons. His arm twitched to throw the useless gun away, but he thought better of it and shoved the pistol into his belt instead. *Maybe we'll be able to use it to figure this transponder thing out later.* The maglev went in three directions from Edinburgh, and two of the platforms held trains. He angled toward the one alerting passengers to its imminent departure and noted only in passing that it was the one he wanted, headed to Inverness, and one step closer to the safety of Azophi Academy.

He dashed through the doors right before they shut and fell into a window seat in an empty row, watching through the glass as his pursuers bounded onto the platform. One raised a pistol to shoot at the train, but he and his allies were already blurring into the background. Jax closed his eyes as adrenaline faded and a wave of pain from his right arm swept over him. *I'll get back to the Academy, Juno can fix me up, and I can ask her out. Perfect plan.*

Athena said, "Jax, most people in the car are staring at you like you're insane. Three are *not* looking in your direction. Increasing tension in their body language suggests they're about to take action."

CHAPTER TWO

Jax didn't give any indication he'd heard the warning, or that he was aware anything at all was amiss. He kept his eyes closed and slumped against the window as if exhausted. *I guess I am exhausted when it comes right down to it. Athena, check the other cars.*

Unlike those he'd ridden previously, this train had three articulated carriages in a row, apparently to accommodate the large number of shuttles that landed in the morning. In any case, it increased the danger but also gave him options, and he definitely needed them. The AI replied, "I have full camera access. I've identified another four people who could be enemy agents based upon their similarity to the others we've seen today."

Don't forget the ones dressed like college students. Neither of us saw those coming.

"Already taken into account."

Okay, let me know when they make their move. Jax had no weapons other than the useless gun, which he could probably throw with some speed in a pinch if he were really desperate. *I'll have to improvise.* Fortunately, improvisation was one of the things he excelled at, one of the things that made him an excellent candidate for the Special Forces position he held. He forced his muscles to relax further, taking as a gift the tiny bit of respite the peaceful interval afforded him. *When things get moving, boost me at need. Like, if I'm injured and can't request it for some reason.*

There was a hint of laughter in the AI's response. "Rest assured that I will do whatever is required to maintain our existence. Whether you expressly give me permission to or not."

A smile quirked the edges of his mouth. *You're one-of-a-kind, Athena.*

"Literally."

Except for the backups. The time for conversation ended as he sensed the enemy agents moving, their actions heralded by the shocked sounds of the other passengers who saw them lurch into motion. Athena's warning came at the same moment, and he snapped his eyes open to find only one between him and the front of the car, meaning that two were coming up from behind. He hoped they wouldn't try shooting in the confined space, but couldn't count on it. Jax ducked below the seatbacks of the row ahead of him, scuttled toward the aisle, then exploded out into it as he ran for the enemies near the rear of the car. *Better one enemy at my back than two.* They all wore identical suits but with differing ties, maybe to demonstrate they were people rather than simply cogs in the Intelligence Division machine. It didn't make Jax feel any better about them.

He crouched slightly, then slammed upward into the

nearest with a forearm block that connected with the other man's crossed arms. It plowed him backward at his partner, the first female agent Jax had seen that day. She stepped nimbly aside into a row of seats as her companion landed on his back, and Jax continued his rush. He put his hands on the high top of the aisle seat in the row in front of the woman, then used his arms as a pivot point to launch himself into a roundhouse kick that took him over and past the prone agent.

She got her fists up to block, but his speed and torque blasted through the defense and pushed her arms back into her head with enough force to bash her skull against the window. It didn't yield since the transparent pane was doubtless made of something tougher than standard glass to endure the train's high velocity, and she sank onto a seat in a daze, her long dark hair half-covering her face. He landed with his feet on the seat beside her and would have paid good money for a moment to lever a punch into her temple and ensure she was out of the fight. Unfortunately, the other members of her team offered him no such opportunity.

The one at the front of the car drew a gun and started shooting. Jax threw himself over the back of the seat and across three rows, then landed hard on the armrests of the fourth. His ribs complained, and his right leg went numb at the impact, but he shrugged off both injuries. *Gotta move, Jax. Go.* He pushed himself into the center aisle in time to take a punch from the man he'd knocked down square on his cheek. Only a last-second swivel saved him from another shot to his broken nose, which would doubtless have compromised his vision again.

He staggered back, and his opponent hesitated for an instant. Jax attributed it to deciding whether to continue hand-to-hand or go for his gun, and the agent dipped a hand under his coat. Jax put his palms on the seatbacks to either side of him and launched himself forward into a leaping kick with a loud shout that distracted the man for a vital beat and knocked him flying again. The weapon dropped to the floor. The agent fell at the feet of the third member of the enemy team, who smirked as he pulled the trigger of the pistol he held at arm's length.

Jax twisted awkwardly to his left, cursing the lack of feeling in his right leg, and couldn't suppress a scream as bullets drilled into his right arm. After the first two, he lost count and any sensation other than agony. *Athena, can you open the door at the back?* The AI didn't reply, but the panel at the rear of the compartment slid aside. Beyond it lay the closed door of the next car back, separated by a jump of at least four feet. He lurched toward it and heard the clatter of a magazine as the man behind him reloaded. He'd lost track of the number of rounds that had struck him.

"Open the other one," he gasped, and the barrier slid aside. It revealed an agent in a dark suit standing beside another imitation college student. Both of them moved toward the front of the car. The only blessing was that they didn't have weapons drawn, but doubtless they would in short order. He felt the cold energy of adrenaline rush through him and ran, leaping easily from one car to the next. A civilian stepped into the aisle directly in his path and forced Jax to slide to a stop. *Athena, close the doors and lock them. Don't let anyone through.*

He shouted in his military command voice, "Everyone

get to the back of the car, now!" and pushed the man in his way to get him moving. He resisted and threw a wide punch at Jax's head. Jax snapped his artificial arm across his body to block since his right wasn't responding to any attempts to convince it to be useful, then gave the man a backhanded slap to the face, just hard enough to convey his seriousness. He growled, "Get your ass moving right now. This is not the moment for misplaced heroism." This time, the other man moved when he pushed.

Jax's foes stood on either side of the aisle in the same row, seemingly content to let the noncombatants clear the path and shoot him. They both suddenly looked quizzical, as if something unexpected was happening. Then they simultaneously holstered their pistols, pulled out batons, and snapped them out full-length to reveal ends that sizzled and crackled.

Athena reported, "They received instructions to capture rather than kill you. They plan to secure the station at Inverness."

He had maybe ten seconds before the path to his enemies would be clear of passengers. *Can the Academy rescue us if we get there?*

"I'll find out."

The bystanders got out of the way, and the faux college kid came forward first. Jax feared that they'd try to pin him against the back of the car where they could each get into a row and strike from two angles, so he advanced to meet him. The other man looked to be about twenty-one years old, was built like a wrestler, and his baton positioning showed he had some familiarity with it. *I don't suppose you figured out the transponder problem on the pistol.*

"I have not. A subroutine is working on it, but without additional research, it seems unlikely I will stumble upon the right frequency and command code."

Okay. Kill the pain from my arm. It's a distraction. The sensation went away, and he narrowed his eyes. His foe swiped the staff horizontally at his skull, and Jax leaned back to let the tip careen past his face with only an inch to spare, compensating for the man's mid-strike arm extension. He offered his opponent a nod. "Nice move. Of course, I saw it coming about a week ago. Do you really think you're good enough to have any chance of beating someone with my experience?"

The other man shrugged. His voice was confident, but not overly so. "You're done, Reese. Whether it's me, my partner, or someone else two weeks from now, you're going down."

Jax nodded again. *Smart, not revealing the surprise waiting at Inverness.* "Do you even know why you're doing this?"

The agent laughed and feinted, which caused Jax to tense up for an instant. "Don't know, and don't care. You're military. You know the rules. They say jump, and you're already in the air before you ask how high."

"I get it. But let me ask you this," then Jax moved. It was occasionally possible to give an opponent a false sense of security by making them think you're having a conversation. Another great strategy was to attack them while *they* were talking. There was something about being human that made one desire the closure of a finished sentence. He rushed the other man, and the baton came across at his head in a forward strike from his right side. Jax stepped forward with his right foot and pivoted, which brought his prosthetic left arm around faster than his rival could've possibly expected. He grabbed the baton's shaft before the stunning tip struck him and continued the spin while levering an elbow into the man's face. As his opponent stumbled backward, Jax lifted his left leg and smashed it straight out backward in a back kick to his foe's sternum that sent him flying. His skull smacked against a pole with a dull *clang*, and he landed bonelessly, clearly out of the fight.

Jax's support leg buckled, and he fell hard on the knee. He pushed the pain away and threw himself into a stumbling run toward the front of the car, where he turned with the baton raised in defense. The other agent, obviously the senior of the two in both age and position, smiled at him. His voice was deeper than the first man's and carried much more accusation and disgust in its tone. "I guess you're all we've been promised. But as the boy said, it doesn't matter. The most painless way for you to handle this would be to let me stun you. Because if you continue to resist, I'm gonna be sure to break a few things that you probably consider important before I put you out." The man backed up into the entryway, where the absence of seats would provide more room for him to maneuver. Unfortunately, unlike his partner, he seemed content to wait Jax out. *Athena, any word on Inverness?*

"A team will be in place to assist as soon as possible, but they likely won't be able to win a straight fight. We'll need to run to reach them. And that agent is between us and the exit."

Jax sighed. *That's always the way, isn't it?* He sauntered toward the middle of the car. At the rear, the passengers were all crowded together with their eyes locked on Jax and his foe. They were the other reason Jax didn't feel comfortable simply waiting until the train reached its destination. If the enemy agent convinced them to assist, Jax could be easily overwhelmed while he did his best not to kill the civilians as they swarmed him. *No, I need to handle this fast.*

He strode forward and flipped the baton around in his hand so it was reversed along his forearm. The other man maintained his forehand grip and steadied himself, centering his balance over his feet while his eyes tracked Jax's approach. His voice was low and confident. "You sure this is how you want to do it?" The grin on his face suggested his preference would be for an affirmative answer.

Jax gave him one. "Less talking, more fighting." He stepped forward and slashed his baton across at a descending diagonal, and the agent skipped backward to avoid it. A rising block deflected a backhand stab with the point, and his foe snapped his baton out at Jax. He slid in and took the blow on the extended elbow of his prosthetic arm while making sure the tip stayed away from him and lashed out with a front kick. The man slapped it aside with a downward strike of his free hand, then grabbed Jax's wrist. His foe yanked at the arm, and Jax pulled in the opposite direction and rotated his palm upward to break the grip.

The hold had been a distraction, and the point of his enemy's baton came up straight at his eyes. Jax bent backward as far as he could, and his right leg failed him again and dropped him onto his back. His enemy swarmed forward and placed his hands on the seatbacks of the nearest row to lever himself into a jump, his feet aimed at Jax's knees. Jax yanked his legs to his chest before the man landed and thrust his heels out at his foe's knees, but the agent was already backpedaling. A baton smashed into his left ankle, and Jax laughed. *Finally, somebody hits the prosthetic.*

He forced himself back to vertical and shook his head. Red spots on the floor caught his eye, and he saw that in addition to hanging uselessly, his right arm was also discharging blood at an alarming rate. *No time to deal with that now, but it does sort of put a clock on this fight, doesn't it?* He flowed into a forward charge with a shout. His opponent stepped into a back stance, then lunged ahead with his baton like a fencer to spear Jax in the chest. With a small prayer that his legs wouldn't fail him, Jax launched himself into the air in a low somersault, swiped down with his prosthetic arm to deflect the baton, and finished the move with a double kick to the man's chest.

His foe went flying, and his baton fell to the floor. He stalked toward the agent, who rose to his feet and reached under his coat for his pistol. Jax shook his head. "Naughty, naughty. Orders are orders." He stepped forward, thrust the stun tip of his baton into his foe's throat, and held it there while the man twitched for a moment before dropping. "Jerk."

He pointed at one of the passengers, an older, gentlemanly looking guy wearing a belt, and ordered, "You, come with me. I need to teach you how to make a tourniquet. As a reward for your assistance, you can help me stun any bad guys who have delusions of adequacy."

CHAPTER THREE

Juno's voice was equal parts disbelief and condescension. "You're a damn fool, Jackson Reese, you know that?"

From his position on the hard table beneath her, he offered her exasperated expression a grin. An all-out dash through the building had followed his arrival at the train station. The agents who had laid in wait had found themselves suddenly blocked or otherwise distracted by undercover operatives from the Academy. Jax had run the gauntlet and burst outside to find a van waiting, and was pretty sure he'd lost consciousness during the leap into the vehicle. He remembered nothing of the drive back to the castle or how he'd wound up in this room. The sight of the articulated robot arms on the ceiling when he finally pried his eyes open led him to the inevitable conclusion that he was in Dr. Juno Cray's medical laboratory. His body was a massive bundle of pain. His right arm throbbed with it, his right leg felt like something was notably amiss, and his skull split as badly as he'd ever felt, probably thanks to the broken nose. He didn't know why painkillers weren't flowing through his veins, but he wasn't a fan.

He ran his tongue across dry lips to wet them. "Nice to see you, too, Doc."

Juno sighed and shook her head. Her long dark hair was pulled back in a ponytail, her perfect skin was free of makeup, and she wore her typical white lab coat over the Academy-standard black trousers and T-shirt. "Honestly, you're a danger to yourself and everyone around you."

Jax chuckled. "Are you referring to my job or to dating me?" He tried to waggle his eyebrows seductively, but her sudden grin suggested he'd failed miserably.

"You're also an idiot." She looked across him, and he turned his head to see an assistant stood on the opposite side of the table. "Help me get him into the scanner." He tensed, expecting they would ask him to try to rise, which wasn't a feat he was confident he could perform. *And one never likes to have performance issues with women they're trying to impress.* He laughed inwardly at his joke.

Athena made a sound very much like a snort. "I think it's fair to assume Dr. Cray has no reason to be impressed with you, regardless of what you do. I still have no idea why she continues to pursue the fiction that you might be suitable romantic partner material. Pity, I'm guessing."

Hush. His right arm jostled as they moved the table suddenly, and he bit down on the moan that attempted to escape. They rolled him to the far end of the room, to the stand-up scanner he'd used before. It slid upward on a track and the long half-cylinder extended to cover his body as Juno and her colleague pushed the table into place. In a slightly muffled voice she ordered, "Remain still. We're going to do a full workup, and it will take fifteen or twenty minutes."

Jax considered the attack he'd faced and what the appropriate response to it might be. Clearly, Zavian Arlox, the head of the UCCA Intelligence Division, had decided that the time for games had passed. Where his moves against Jax and the Academy had previously been subtle, now he was blatantly trying to sweep the board clean. *Pretty inconvenient for the pieces, I'd say.*

Athena agreed. "Speaking as one of them, I would prefer that you took a little better care of yourself in the future."

Can't promise anything, I'm afraid. There was no way to tell when the next attack would come, but it was now more or less guaranteed that if they didn't end Arlox, eventually, Arlox would end them. He wasn't sure who their enemy might target, but it certainly included the people at the Academy, Jax, Major Anika Stephenson, and probably Jax's Special Forces unit as well. All of them were aware to a greater or lesser degree of the government official's actions. That made their continued existence a threat to his power and authority, which clearly couldn't stand.

Athena observed, "Also, likely the people you have relied upon during your missions. Lady Elle for one, possibly the Reardens, for another."

Dammit, you're right. He shook his head slightly, and a stern "Stop moving" came from beyond the sensor shield. *The real question is, what are we going to do about it?* It was virtually impossible to get to Arlox, or at least Jax certainly had no idea how he might accomplish such a thing. The man was paranoid, and with good reason given his role as spymaster for the Alliance. Both the Confederacy and the Alien Coalition would throw celebrations were he to meet an untimely demise. Jax was sure that most of the people who'd encountered Arlox probably felt the same way. He'd met similar personalities in the military, and they were far from beloved. *Yep, I'm at a loss on this one.*

Athena replied, "Well, it's good that you tend to surround yourself with people smarter than you, then. Perhaps the Professor, or Dr. Cray, or Cia, or maybe even one of the groundskeeping robots can give you some ideas."

Aww, you're the only robot I listen to, so there's no need to worry about being replaced by another. He knew that being called a robot irritated her, so he tried to work it into their conversation as often as he could. He was ruminating on how to kill someone as well-hidden as Arlox when the canopy rose to reveal Juno staring down at him. She wore a frown, the kind he'd seen on doctors' faces before that signals bad news to come. He nodded solemnly. "Give it to me straight, Doc. It's a fatally broken heart, right? Try not to feel *too* guilty for not asking me out before such a tragic event occurred."

She rolled her eyes. "If only it were something so simply remedied. No, I have two important pieces of information to share. The first is that you are now completely wired."

A male voice entered the conversation unexpectedly. Professor Nikolai Maarsen said, "What's that? The AI has spread its influence fully through him?"

Juno nodded. "Athena has been using biological material to create connections from her core in his brain throughout his body. The expansion speed seems to have increased beyond our baseline projections. I would've expected only about two-thirds coverage by now, based on our last evaluation." She lowered her head to look at him. "Athena, would you care to explain?"

A nearby monitor flickered, then the image of the artificial intelligence's avatar appeared upon it. She had long blonde hair swept over to one side, thin eyebrows, and a wide smile. Her voice indicated no regret, chagrin, reluctance, or anything similar about the situation. "Of course, Dr. Cray. Jax has received an unexpectedly large amount of quick heal drugs in the past few weeks. Due to this, I have been able to accelerate the spread of my connections. That, combined with the ability to boost his endorphins and chemical balance to make his body's acceptance of the changes smoother, has made it possible to roughly double the speed with which I could construct the lines."

Maarsen sounded both thoughtful and unworried. "Now that you have the connections, what do you intend to do with them?" It was a potentially loaded question. Jax generally tried not to think about the fact that he harbored a being in his head who might have its own agenda. Whenever the notion crossed his mind, he pushed any consideration of it away since there was nothing he could do about it. His passenger was too deeply embedded in his brain tissue to remove her without killing him. But if he had become the AI's tool, that particular undesired outcome might no longer be a sufficient deterrent when weighed against the need to control her.

Athena seemed to understand the unspoken concern. "Only what I've been doing so far, Professor, but better. I can increase the speed of his muscular response when necessary, I can control blood flow better than I have before, and I can now use all his senses to a higher degree than I was previously able."

Juno asked bluntly, "Can you make him do things he doesn't want to do?"

A slight hesitation preceded Athena admitting, "Yes, but not effectively or efficiently. Even with all of my processing power, I cannot match the throughput required to operate a human body. There's too much going on simultaneously. I can make the legs move, but I cannot maintain balance as well as Jax. I can swing the arm, but I cannot target it as effectively as we could together. We are better thought of as symbiotes, rather than as one being in control and another subordinate."

Jax added, "I don't feel like a zombie if that's any help."

Juno and the Professor replied together, "It's not." The doctor continued, "What safeguards do we have against the possibility that you're lying to us, and have become some sort of danger?"

Athena's tone didn't change. "You have none. The options are the same as they were from the beginning. However, there is no safe way to remove me without killing Jax. I could survive, but I presume if you removed me, I wouldn't be re-implanted in a human, which is my fundamental purpose. To be honest, I find the current arrangement rewarding and have no desire to alter it." A note of hopefulness entered her voice and reminded him how much her verbal communication had improved since their meeting. "Unless, of course, a more intelligent host with the same physical aptitudes was available."

Jax groaned, and the other two laughed. Juno said, "Okay, let's put a pin in that conversation for now. I have bad news, Jax. We couldn't save your arm. It'll have to be removed and replaced."

He nodded. "I figured that it was probably done for when I no longer felt pain from the bullets hitting it. Do what you gotta do, Doc."

She nodded, brusque and businesslike, and looked up at the others in the room. "Okay. Let's put him out." The robot arms whirred, a cold needle bit into his neck, and he knew no more.

―――――

Jax awoke in a darkened medical lab to find Juno seated in the chair next to him, reading. A self-assessment revealed that all the pain had vanished, and he took a moment to savor the relief of its absence. He coughed. "How did it go?"

She closed her book and stood. "Take a look for yourself." Long fingers pulled back the sheet that covered him to show his right arm, which was still a skeletal array of metal and fiber. The skin graft was creeping in from the spot where the mechanical piece met the portion of his human arm that remained. He saw something strange that he didn't recognize near the top and pointed at it. "What's that?"

Juno replied, "That's Athena."

Really?

The artificial intelligence replied, "Yes. It's much easier to create the line before all the additional biological matter has filled in. You'll have more strength and precision with this arm than you do with the other one.

He looked up at Juno. "Advanced model, eh?"

She nodded. "Top-of-the-line technology. Better than anyone else has. I think you're going to like it."

Athena observed, "You know, if you got the rest of your limbs replaced, we would be significantly faster and stronger. Just putting that out there."

I like those pieces, thanks. My mother gave them to me. He grinned at Juno. "So, about that heartbreak?"

She laughed and patted him on the shoulder. "Once you heal up, and once you find the time since I think you're going to be busy, maybe you should try asking me out again. It's your turn." She turned and headed from the room. Jax admired her retreating form and wondered if there was a way to take down Arlox immediately, so he could get on to what was *really* important.

Athena made a disgusted sound. "Honestly. I don't know what she sees in you."

Jax closed his eyes and relaxed. *I don't either. I'm just glad she does.*

CHAPTER FOUR

After being discharged and taking the time to shower and change into the Academy's black uniform, Jax strode intently toward Maarsen's office. The Professor's message had indicated in no uncertain terms that he required Jax's presence immediately. He entered the space, again noting the comfortable environment that reflected the personality of the man behind the desk. It had a sort of casual formality, the fireplace comfortable rather than fancy, the bookshelves inviting rather than ornamental.

Maarsen himself was in his usual suit and shirt without a tie and had slicked his longish grey hair back out of the way. His mustache, beard, and sideburns all looked like they could use a little attention, and his green eyes seemed to be more sunken in their sockets than usual. He looked more concerned than Jax recalled seeing him, his normally genial face wearing a slight frown. His voice, however, still retained its characteristic warmth. "Jackson, good to see you up and about. How's the arm?"

He lifted the limb and waved it around a little to

demonstrate that it was fully functional. "From what I hear, it'll be much better than the original."

Maarsen nodded. "We can use any advantage we can get at this point. Grab yourself a drink and take a seat." It was only early afternoon, but Jax wasn't about to refuse. He poured himself a modest amount of the amber whiskey from the decanter and settled into the right-hand chair. Maarsen said, "Activate," and a holographic display materialized over his desk. It showed a view of the Earth from space, with time accelerated to show the planet spinning slowly. *I haven't seen that image before. Wonder if it means the Professor is occupied with concerns of global importance?*

Athena offered, "The fight against Zavian Arlox could be considered a universal problem."

No argument there. The man was doing backroom deals with aliens and the Confederacy, doubtless all in the name of Alliance security. *Or at least that's what he'd say to anyone who found out.* Somehow, Jax doubted that was his only motivation or even his primary one. *Once people like that have power, they want more and more and more.*

Maarsen ordered, "Connect to Anika." There was a brief pause, during which the older man stared expectantly at the display, then the scowling face of Major Anika Stephenson appeared.

"What can I do for you, Nikolai?"

The Professor grinned, and there was genuine affection in the expression. "I have your favorite subordinate with me. You've been informed of his recent adventures, yes?"

Stephenson's scowl grew deeper. "I have. And I think he needs to keep his eyes open better."

Jax snorted. "It was like thirty-seven on one."

Athena corrected, "It was at best ten on one."

Hush. Stephenson shook her head. "Regardless. You should have anticipated the attack. We *all* should have."

Maarsen nodded. "Fortunately, we already had the defenses in place for the team that came after me, and the one that tried for Dr. Cray." Jax's eyes snapped up from staring at his glass. He hadn't heard that they'd targeted Juno. He wondered if she knew. The Professor continued, "We will continue to maintain those defenses. But it would be far better, Anika, if you were here with us. You, and to a lesser extent Jackson's Special Forces comrades, are in danger."

She shook her head. "I have several things to wrap up before I can legitimately take leave. If I depart with them undone, it will be a red flag to our enemies."

Jax suggested, "Maybe keep Lyton with you at all times?"

Stephenson snorted. "No, he's too valuable where he is."

Maarsen let out a small sigh. "I don't like to disagree with you, but you're remaining in a very unsafe situation for no clear gain. Our enemies are already aware we're onto them, as evidenced by the first wave of attacks."

The major ran her hands through her short-cropped blonde hair. "I know. But here's the thing. There might be a good reason for me to stay where I am. I have connections I won't be able to use if I'm away on leave. People who can give us a heads-up about what the Intelligence Division is up to. It might be better to remain on the *Cronus*. It's not like I'm an easy target when I'm on board."

Jax replied, "All the more reason to keep Lyton with you at all times. Come on. He's fun."

She chuckled. "He is most certainly *not* fun. In fact, he's downright annoying, almost equal to your level of accomplishment in that area. That's why I put him on your team." She paused for a moment as if thinking, and continued, "But I suppose I do need an aide. And if that aide also happens to be a highly-skilled bodyguard, that's not something anyone else needs to be aware of."

Maarsen drummed his fingers on the desk, then shrugged. "You know your situation best, Anika. I'll leave the decision to you, naturally, since I don't have any other option. I still believe you would be safer here."

She laughed. "Oh, no question. But it's not exactly my job to be safe."

"Speaking of unsafe, Jackson, you'll be interested to know that Gretchen Paltar was allegedly killed by the Confederacy a couple of days ago," Maarsen added.

Jax blinked in surprise. "Really? That's unexpected." She was Arlox's minion. Jax had unsuccessfully tried to compromise her, which resulted in a lot of physical and mental pain.

Maarsen shrugged. "Arlox is cleaning house. He tried to kill his principal enemies with hunter teams, and he wiped out the best trail leading back to him. On the upside, we've got him worried."

"Are you sure it was him behind it, not something coincidental?" He didn't believe it was a coincidence but figured the question had to be asked.

The Professor somberly shook his head. "Had it only been her, I suppose I might've considered that a possibility. However, her home also exploded and demolished the ones to either side and caused several deaths."

Jax winced. "Not exactly subtle, is he?"

Stephenson snorted. "He's never been in the same room with subtle, at least where vengeance is concerned. One must assume he's pretty accomplished at misdirection in other areas, given his position."

He changed the subject. "So, Arlox needs to go down. How are we going to do it? Blow up a ship in transit? You have favors you can call in with Captain Jensen of the *Cronos*, right Major?"

A single laugh escaped Maarsen. "Nothing so grand is available, I'm afraid. The man stays on the move, which makes placing any sort of trap almost impossible. Without knowing where he is, the only option would be to drive him to us somehow, which carries excessive danger and likely wouldn't work. He'd send endless teams of underlings before he'd get personally involved."

Stephenson asked, "Any political opponents we can leverage?"

Maarsen sighed. "Had you sought that information a day ago, I would have said there was one in a reasonable position to mount a challenge. However, that individual died in their sleep last night."

She growled, "Probably not natural causes, huh? This guy is a class-A bastard."

Jax asked, *Athena, any ideas?*

The AI replied, "If we cannot bring him to us, we must go to him. Which means we must find a way to know where he's going to be. We need a spy in his organization who knows his travel plans."

He echoed her comments to the others, and Maarsen agreed. "That would be the easiest solution, but he's surrounded himself with exceedingly loyal people. We can't assume there's any trust there. He doubtless has them under near-constant surveillance."

Stephenson nodded. "So, what we need to do is separate one of those people from his protection and have a conversation with them." Her emphasis on the word conversation made it clear she wasn't talking about a comfortable chat over drinks.

Jax shrugged. "Okay. Been there, done that, got the T-shirt. Who's the target?"

Maarsen instructed, "Photo, please," and Stephenson's image slid to one side. A low-quality surveillance photo of a mousy looking man with an expression of concern on his face joined it. Jax idly wondered whether Maarsen's system was smart enough to know what he was referring to, whether he preset the picture before the meeting, or if there was a human listening in to give him what he requested. The older man interrupted his musings. "Quentin Foster is Arlox's primary assistant. We've been able to identify a couple of other people in his network, but this one holds the unique position of being an only child who appears to care deeply for his parents."

Jax said, "So, we have a source of leverage on this guy. How do we use it?"

Maarsen shrugged. "If our objective is to get one of Arlox's people out of his immediate protective circle, this is the only one we know of with a vulnerability. His parents live in a smallish dome city on Mars, which puts them within our sphere of influence."

Jax replied, "I know you're not talking about interrogating the parents since he'd never have made it as Arlox's assistant if he were loose-lipped. So, we have to use them to draw him there. False message?"

Stephenson shook her head. "They'd be smart enough to figure that out, I'm sure. It has to be real. I hate to say this, but we may have to inconvenience his folks a little."

Maarsen nodded. "A health crisis would do it. Nothing fatal, but something that presented as serious enough that it might be."

Jax sighed. "This is a pretty long shot."

Stephenson replied, "We've had longer."

The Professor added, "If you have other ideas, any at all, now is the time to put them forward."

Jax paused a minute to see if Athena would give him something, but she remained silent. "I agree. We put the parents in apparent danger to bring our target to Mars, where my team and I will take care of him. Any reason to wait?" They shook their heads, again in tandem. "All right. I guess tomorrow we're on the way to Mars."

CHAPTER FIVE

The ride to the airfield northeast of the Academy was comfortably familiar. Cia met him at breakfast, and they headed up before the rest of the team, filling the drive with enjoyable conversation peppered with sarcastic snaps from the pilot. *When she finds out who's coming along on this trip, she's never going to let me live it down.*

Athena replied, "It does seem awfully convenient."

Shut it. It wasn't my idea. To be honest, I'm not completely thrilled about it. Really, it's your fault.

"Since I was part of the tracker's development, I suppose I can't argue. But I don't know if Dr. Cray's presence with the crew for this mission is strictly essential."

Jax gave a small laugh. *You clearly never tried to stop her from doing something she has her mind set on.* To Cia, he said, "So, been keeping busy?"

She didn't take her eyes off the road. "The usual. Ferry people here and there, deliver things from here to there, and from there to here. As usual, as long as I get to fly, I'm happy." Her pale skin seemed brighter than usual, which led him to think she'd dyed her short hair a deeper shade of black. "Of course, I'm always happiest when I'm working with you, Jax." The sarcastic drawl in her voice was impossible to miss.

He laughed. "Oh, I very much feel the same, don't doubt it. Really, the only thing that makes dealing with your nonsense tolerable is that the *Grace* is such a good ship." She made a noise of agreement as she pulled the van to a stop a distance from their ride. It was in its normal configuration, with the musical note that was its only obvious decoration standing out prominently on the hull near the nose. The side hatch was open, and they climbed up the ladder to it while workers bustled out of a nearby building to move their cargo from the vehicle into the ship. They were traveling comparatively light since the mission ahead was more about subtlety than direct conflict.

He was completing preflight checks in the pilot's compartment with Cia when he got a surprise. Trianna entered and growled, "Move." It was the most he'd heard from the Academy's other pilot, who made a point of not talking to anyone she didn't like. It appeared he was still on that list. He obeyed with a grin and a quick slap on Cia's shoulder and headed to the back. The rest of the crew put the final restraining straps on the storage crates and closed up the cargo door. He traded handshakes and fist bumps with the team, including Juno, and said to her, "Allow me to escort you to your lift-off position."

She shook her head and gave him a look of disappointment, hopefully feigned. "Not my first trip, Jax. Not even my first trip on the *Grace*." She strode past him, headed for the front of the ship. Kenton Marshall shook his head. "You're smooth, man. *Super* smooth."

Jax lifted his eyes to the ceiling as if beseeching the universe for justice. "One day, someone on this team is going to show me an iota of respect. I tell you, one day, it will happen."

Ethan Kimmel, the youngest-looking member of the team and the one most likely to be mistaken for a ghost with his pale skin and blonde hair, replied, "Probably posthumously. Yeah, definitely posthumously."

Laughter ruled the moment as Jax followed the others forward and strapped in for takeoff. Once they were safely *en route* to Mars, Cia abandoned her piloting duties to join the rest of the crew, who had gathered around the table in the galley as usual. It wasn't big enough for all of them, so Jax and Cia stood with their backs to the cabinets while the rest filled the available chairs. He made the appropriate introductions, but everyone was familiar with Juno, and she with them.

He cleared his throat to attract their attention. "Okay. This mission is a little weird, even for us. Our target is Zavian Arlox's assistant, and we need to pull him out of the Intelligence Division's protective circle so we can get a shot at him." He wasn't willing to share all the information about exactly what form that shot would take quite yet.

Athena snickered, "Shot. You made a joke. Because it's an injection. You're coming right along."

Shut it. "So, our boy Quentin is the dutiful only son of a lovely pair of elderly parents on Mars. We're heading there now to create a reason for him to come back for a visit."

Maria Verrand said, "Not a funeral, I hope." Her voice

was neutral, but of them all, she would've probably been the most willing to take such extreme measures given that Arlox and his people had blackmailed her into compromising the team in the past. Her long brown hair, always neatly braided, was now pulled back severely. Her face carried a tension that hadn't been there when they'd met, and he regretted his part in putting it there.

Jax shook his head. "Nothing quite so dramatic, although a health crisis and a hospital visit is part of the plan."

Anton Sirenno, the tall, dark, and handsome member of the team, looked uncomfortable. "I'll do a lot of things for the Academy, but I'm not sure that putting the beatdown on senior citizens is within my current definition of acceptable behavior."

Cia rolled her eyes and quipped, "Please. If the right woman fluttered her pretty eyelashes at you, your alleged morals would disappear like that." She snapped her fingers.

Sirenno chuckled. "Well, I see three potential flutterers in the room. Anyone volunteering?"

Cia replied, "Eww." Verrand and Juno laughed.

Jax resolved the issue with a grin. "No, we're not going to do them lasting physical injury. Juno and Athena have come up with something that mimics real symptoms but isn't ultimately dangerous. It will send them to the hospital and confuse the doctors enough that they should feel the need to call our target home."

Kimmel countered, "And if they don't?"

Jax shrugged. "We'll do it ourselves. We expect the parents will have ordinary civilian comms, which Athena should easily crack to get emergency contact codes for their son. After that, it's as simple as making the source appear to be the hospital and transmitting the call. Then, if he calls back, he'll get confirmation from them that they're there."

The others nodded. Cia asked, "And after he's on his way?"

Jax shook his head. "That end of the plan is still in development, so we'll hold off on discussing it until we've succeeded with the first part. How long until we get to Mars?"

She shrugged. "We're taking the slow way around, so about half a day."

Kimmel asked, "Are we going to visit your parents again?"

Cia's scowl was impressive. "I certainly hope not."

Jax laughed. "Maybe we can stop by if we have time when we've finished, but the city we're headed to is half a planet away from the Rearden estate."

Juno commented, "Pity. I've heard so many good things."

The pilot barked a laugh. "About the estate, sure. About the people who live there, well, if you heard good things, someone's been lying to you."

There was a round of laughter, and Cia wandered forward to resume her piloting duties. Jax looked at the crew, all of whom wore smirks of one kind or another and carefully didn't meet his gaze, and rolled his eyes. "Okay, get it out of your systems."

Verrand was first. "So, Juno, you're slumming, is that it? Or is it pity dating?"

Sirenno added, "I think pity dating is the most likely

reason. Or, you're simply so bored from the lack of options at the Academy that Jax, for some insane, incomprehensible reason, looks good to you. Let me tell you; you can do better."

Marshall offered, "If you want to date someone other than him, for the sake of comparison, I'm certainly willing to take you out to dinner." Verrand and Sirenno echoed the offer.

Kimmel, who carried a not-so-secret torch for Cia, bobbed his head. "I'm sure that Cia or Trianna can find you someone better, or at least someone whose, uh, intellectual abilities are at least as fully developed as their physical capabilities."

Juno laughed with a broad smile but didn't reply. Jax said, "You all wound me. Deeply. If you weren't so predictable, I might even be hurt. Now, go rest or do whatever the hell it is you people do with your free time. Juno and I have some training to do."

Verrand lifted an eyebrow. "That's what you're calling it nowadays?"

Sirenno said, "Aha. That explains it. It's not pity, so much as she saw how deficient he is and feels the need to help him improve his courtship skills and such. Definitely an appropriate doctor move." Jax didn't reply, only waved at Juno, and led her into the training area in the back.

When they arrived and were finally alone, he said, "So, it seems like pity is the consensus."

She shook her head. "I'll never tell."

"You, too? The universe is such a cruel, cruel place." He shook his head and dropped out of flirty mode. "I don't think it's likely that we'll find ourselves in any fights, at least not if we do our jobs right. If combat does occur, your main plan should be to get to the back and let the overly physical people like me, Marshall, and Verrand handle it. But, I thought we could go through some simple locks, blocks, and escapes in case."

She nodded. "I have some martial arts experience, but certainly nothing like what you all have."

"Any foundation is better than no foundation, generally speaking. So, let me see you deliver a punch with your dominant arm." He stepped into a back stance, and she did the same before advancing and throwing a slow cross with her right hand. Jax lifted his left arm and intercepted it. "Okay, now watch this." He slid his block down to grab her wrist, then twisted it and brought it across his body, which forced her to bend over from the pain of the locked-out joint. He did it slowly enough that it was neither damaging nor particularly painful. "What do you do?"

Juno pivoted on her front foot and tried a back kick with her left. Jax circled out of the way and maintained the lock. "Good instinct, but won't work. Once I have you like this, you're pretty much toast. Let's go back and try it again." They repeated the punch and block, and this time as he grabbed her wrist, he instructed, "Now, strike my hold away with your left fist before I can establish it."

She correctly delivered a blow with the bottom of her fist, not the knuckles, and forced him to release his grip. He nodded. "Good. Good work. Now, same thing with the other side."

They practiced it several times, then Juno observed, "Your right arm is faster."

Jax, always cool and suave, replied, "Huh?"

She laughed. "The new prosthetic is faster than the old one. That makes sense, as the muscle fibers are more advanced. But it also suggests Athena is as fully integrated with the new limb as with the other."

Jax spoke out loud. "Athena, is that true?"

The voice in his head replied, "It is. I'm now fully connected and am learning how best to complement your movements. Sometimes it's a little extra speed, and sometimes it's assistance with aim. But all our efforts so far have shown that we're better working together than you are working alone."

"Athena agrees with you and says we're more than the sum of our parts."

Juno laughed. "Interesting way to put it, but yes, that sounds right. Do you have any negative side effects, physical or mental?"

"None that I'm aware of, although I could've used a longer rehabilitation time under the direct care of a doctor, I think. Perhaps once this is all over, we can rectify that on a resort planet. I've been to one, and it was nice. Might be fun to be there for pleasure instead of business. I mean, for health reasons, rather than business."

She lifted an eyebrow. "So you can streak through the place naked again?"

Jax groaned. "I wasn't naked, and it was a role I played for the mission."

"Sure it was. You keep saying that. Also, a little talk therapy might not be a bad thing for you."

"Okay, whatever, smartass. Let's get on with the practice."

CHAPTER SIX

They landed at a spaceport that served several small domed cities and took a train into the one that was the home to Quentin's parents. Jax dispatched Kimmel and Sirenno to secure a hotel room, and the remainder of the team headed for the city's main commercial area.

Athena, have you found them?

"They're still in position at the restaurant."

Normally he would have devoted more time to watch the pair and find the perfect moment to make his move. But the AI had spotted them on the city's ubiquitous cameras during their descent, out in the open for an afternoon of shopping. That would've made an immediate strike an appealing option in its own right, but when Mr. and Mrs. Foster moved to a local café and took a seat at an outdoor table, the opportunity was far too optimal to pass up. *Okay, vector us in.*

The café was crowded, with only one outside table still unoccupied. Verrand and Marshall secured it while Juno, Cia, and Jax stayed around a corner a block away. He slipped on his display glasses, and Athena fed him an image of the scene from the nearby cameras. Quentin's parents were spry and healthy-looking. The data the Academy had pulled indicated they were in their early fifties, which meant they must've had their child pretty young. Jax pictured them playing tennis, or on the golf course, or doing some other couples-friendly recreational activity that got them outside and exercising. *They seem the type. I wonder if Mars has golf courses?* He snuck a glance at Juno and thought, *Maybe that'll be us one day.*

Athena snorted. "At the moment our chances of survival aren't conducive to imagining such a future. Plus, there's no way this relationship is going to work out. She's too smart for you."

Hush. Since we're symbiotes and all, how about you make me smarter, then?

"Impossible. You lack the raw potential."

He shook his head in defeat and focused on the image again. The couple was eating, and each had a pair of beverages, one positioned above and to each side of their plates. Their original plan had been to shoot dissolvable capsules at them with the small air pistol hidden in Jax's pocket. But the situation that presented itself now offered different, more precise possibilities.

He said, "How about this? Cia goes up and creates a scene with Verrand and Marshall, and we use the distraction to spike their drinks."

Juno nodded. "Jilted lover. An affair, I think."

Cia laughed softly. "With which one?"

He grinned. "Your choice. Whoever will make it more dramatic."

She tapped a finger against her chin thoughtfully. "Marshall, I think. I don't want to mess up Verrand's pretty face by punching it."

On the camera that showed the café, Maria Verrand smiled, and Kenton Marshall gave a small scowl. Jax hadn't been concerned about anyone hacking their comms here, so everyone wore a transparent earpiece connected to their wrist devices so they could hear the rest. Jax added, "Juno and I can be lovers out for a stroll."

The woman in question raised an eyebrow. "Oh, you think, do you?" Her tone was just frosty enough to *almost* be real, and it drew a laugh from Jax and Cia and smiles from the others. "I don't have a better plan, though, so we'll hope everyone understands that I'm with you out of pity."

Jax shook his head and put a palm over his heart while mouthing the word "Ouch." Then he tapped Cia on the shoulder. "No time like the present."

She wandered around the corner and walked down the street while idly peering into the windows of the stores on the right. The moment when she supposedly spotted her alleged partner in the romantic triangle was obvious. Her body stiffened, she paused for a second, then strode forward with growing agitation. Jax commented, "Our turn," and offered Juno his arm. She linked her left through it, the two tiny capsules that would dissolve when they touched liquid palmed in the other. Fortunately, Juno and Athena had planned for several possibilities, so they already had the liquid version of the capsules in addition to the gun's ammunition. It was a given that the doctor had the best hands for the operation, so she'd be the one to deploy the drug.

Jax increased their pace a little as the pilot reached the table and screamed, "You bastard!" She smacked Marshall with an open hand that dumped him onto the pavement, his chair tipping over to one side. *A little overacting, but whatever works.* Every head turned, and every eye locked on the unfolding drama. Cia stood over him and shouted about how he said he was leaving his wife, all the promises he'd made, and what about the baby?

Jax kept a steady pace as he guided Juno past Quentin's parents, who both stared at the scene. Marshall had fallen inward toward the restaurant, drawing everyone's gaze away from their path near the street, and it was a simple matter for Juno to drop the small pellets into the Fosters' glasses. They continued walking as they blatantly looked at the commotion with disdainful expressions and loudly discussed the weirdos yelling at each other. Verrand rose to her feet, then shouted and pointed at both Cia and Marshall, the latter still sprawled on the ground under the continuing barrage of insults from the pilot. Finally, Cia quit yelling, and Jax's display showed her following them down the block. They turned the corner and waited, and she joined them with a grin.

Athena noted, "The restaurant called the authorities. We should move." Verrand had prepaid, as they always did when in the field, so the duo could leave the table without a problem, still shouting at one another as they headed in different directions.

Jax grinned at the sight. "A success. A definite success. Let's get to the hotel."

It was Juno's turn to steer as they made their way to their home base on the planet. Jax kept his eyes glued to the view of the outside of the café. The parents had gone back to their meals and shook their heads as they talked. Each of them drank from the spiked glasses several times. He narrated the scene to the others, including the ones waiting at the hotel, as they walked. After about ten minutes, as the Fosters lingered over coffee, the man suddenly put a hand on his chest and went pale. A waiter bustled over immediately and lifted his fingers to the headset he wore. Athena said, "Medics have been called."

Jax shared that information with the rest, and Juno nodded in satisfaction at the quick response. He said, "Good, we don't have to make the call ourselves. One less thread leading back to us." Although they were all confident Athena could effectively spoof the call, it was always better not to need the tricks, for fear that some random chance would intervene to their detriment. The woman reacted to the drug moment later as she also grabbed her chest and slumped in her chair. The waiter knelt beside her and held her steady, and the medics arrived shortly after.

When he shared the information, Juno observed, "Good response time."

Athena said, "I called in a fake report to draw them near beforehand."

Jax frowned. *Are you sure that was smart? Or, do you think that was smart to do without informing the rest of us?*

"The risk was minimal, the reward high, and I consider it my job to improve our chances where I can. Besides, you were busy with your end of the operation."

We're going to talk about this.

"No, we're not. Because when you think about it, you'll realize that if you had thought of it first, you would've asked me to do it." Jax blinked in surprise as the AI continued, "The medics are taking them in. They called ahead for a team of doctors to be waiting."

Jax said, "Okay people, they're on the way to the hospital, which means Phase One is complete. Let's get to the hotel and work on Phase Two."

———

By the time the team had checked into their rooms, the call had gone out from the hospital to Quentin. He'd said he would be there within a day, and they'd told him to hurry. Everything was going exactly to plan.

They'd split up for a while, Jax taking the opportunity to rest while he could, then met as duos and trios for a meal in the hotel's restaurant, making sure not to arrive or leave at the same time. Their cover was as competitors for a business contract who were in town to visit a corporation. The meetings were already scheduled, and as before, other Academy students or staff would show up for them if his team was unavailable. If everything went right, they'd be off-planet before it happened.

Now, they were gathered in his mini-suite to plan for the next day's operation. He'd gotten the largest room available, which featured the separate living area that held couches, chairs, and a small table, all of them currently occupied by him and his team. Athena had confirmed that their target's parents were stable but still critical, as they'd expected. Jax remarked, "That's some impressive stuff you came up with, Juno."

She nodded. "I couldn't have done it without Athena. She has a lot of useful information stored away."

Athena, who had taken over the room's screen to display her avatar after ensuring all the interior surveillance was nullified, replied, "Nor I without you, Dr. Cray. Once again, we're greater than the sum of our parts."

Jax requested, "Athena, bring us up to speed."

Her representation, which wore her blonde hair short today and had on a silver necklace and what looked like the lapels of a suit covering her shoulders, nodded. "Our target has checked in twice already. The communications are encoded and routed through multiple systems, so I can't locate him, but he says he will arrive tomorrow morning."

Cia whistled. "Either he wasn't very far away, or he has a seriously fast ship."

Kimmel shrugged. "We're probably lucky he wasn't already on Mars when the call went out."

Jax growled, "The inability to know where the hell Arlox is at any given moment is a source of great frustration to me." The others laughed and confirmed that it was to them, as well.

Athena continued, "In any case, we have confirmation that he's on the way. I've located the Intelligence Division agents present in this city. According to the Academy's information, there are only two, and I have surveillance on them through the city's systems. Both are currently at home."

Jax said, "I think it's safe to assume that one or both of them will be our boy's handler tomorrow. Pick him up, take him to the hospital, keep an eye on him, that sort of thing. We need to make sure that doesn't happen."

Sirenno cracked his knuckles. "Now, I wouldn't mind putting the beatdown on them, assuming that they're not also senior citizens."

Verrand replied, "I'm in as well, but knocking them around does seem a little less than subtle."

Jax nodded. "We have a couple of different options. First, Kimmel here can try, along with Athena, to provide some misinformation that suggests he's arriving later than he should. That would be the simplest solution, and probably the least easily traced back to us."

Cia frowned. "Why Ethan? Can't Athena handle that herself?"

Jax smothered the grin that wanted to reach his lips. *I guess maybe that torch goes in both directions.* Athena explained, "It's likely that given the encryption on their comms, any attempt to send misinformation will need to happen from short range."

Kimmel nodded. "Basically, we can't get through on the main line, but all comms, even ours, have a near field connection. I might be able to lock onto that. If I can, Athena can use my comm as a repeater to do the work."

Jax added, "Before you ask, no, Athena can't be the local one. I need to be there for our move against Quentin."

Cia frowned. "And if the misdirection isn't successful?"

"I'm pretty sure this is when the whole 'being part of a team' thing becomes valuable. Who has a plan?"

Marshall said, "Well, Arlox already knows the Academy is onto him, and Mars is pretty close to Earth. What if Cia, Sirenno, Verrand, and I make ourselves obvious? Those two post outside the agents' homes so they notice they're being watched, and Cia and I go to the next town over and do the same with the agents there. That should keep them inside, at least long enough to call back for instructions, which should be plenty of time for us to make our move. Worst case, we neutralize their vehicles if they try to head out."

Jax drummed his fingers on the table he shared with Cia and Kimmel. The others had scattered around the living room on the couches and comfortable chairs. "I don't love it, but I also don't have a better option. At least with a visible presence in more than one city, it might leave some uncertainty about what's going on. Any arguments against?"

None were forthcoming, so Jax announced, "It's done, then. Everyone have a good night's sleep, except for Cia and Kenton, who will head on over to Tramal and settle in there. Athena, please contact the Academy and have them book rooms and a cover story."

The avatar nodded. "On it."

Jax smiled. "Okay, all of you get out of my room. No carousing or spending the night on the town. We need to be ready to go first thing in the morning, in case we discover that our boy Quentin has some surprises up his sleeve."

CHAPTER SEVEN

Jax had realized shortly after they'd broken up the night before that he would need another person for the pickup in case something went wrong, and Cia was the one he trusted most. That left Trianna to go along with Marshall in her place. Jax had fallen asleep laughing about the notion that they'd pass the entire trip in silence. Athena, of course, had suggested that since the other man wasn't nearly as big an idiot as Jax, that their backup pilot would probably enjoy talking with him.

So it was Cia who helped him steal a van with dark-tinted windows from one of the car companies that serviced the airport, and she was now in the driver's seat to his left. They'd snagged a uniform for her as well, and he thought she looked very snappy in the navy blue trousers and button-down shirt. The chauffeur's hat was the perfect finishing touch, and one he planned never to let her forget.

Juno was on the bench seat behind them, with a back-pack holding the essential supplies for the mission at her feet. With luck, the company wouldn't notice the vehicle's loss until much later in the day. The rest of the team had signaled as they arrived at their assignments, and while Athena could have provided him with imagery of each, he'd opted to stay focused on his immediate surroundings. Reports came in over the comms. First the watchers getting into place, then Kimmel attempting his hack against the two agents, each of whom lived in the same section of the town. The computer expert muttered, "Not great operational security, that decision."

Jax observed, "No, but people are creatures of habit, even spies. They would want to be reasonably close to their workplace, especially since they might be called to it in a hurry, given their career choice." The two had settled on opposite sides of the disguised Intelligence Division headquarters, which was a better alternative than if they'd lived together or in the same neighborhood. But the criticism wasn't wrong, and Jax hoped that he'd choose more wisely if presented with such a requirement.

After several moments, Kimmel made a disgusted sound. "I can't get linked up. They've got the near field connection protected, too."

Jax sighed. "Well, that's why we have backup plans, right? Stay in place, in case we need you to assist the others."

Athena warned, "Another call to the hospital. He says he's landed." While she wasn't able to crack Quentin's encoded comm, getting into the hospital's system had been the work of only a moment. She and Juno had checked on the Fosters' records that morning, and both were convinced the pair would be fine in a day or two. Juno said,

"We should send them an anonymous gift afterward to make up for their trouble."

Before Jax could reply, Athena said, "On it," over the comm.

He shook his head. Adding the AI to the communication channel felt strange but somehow comforting as if she wasn't only a part of him anymore. He pushed the thought away. The whole thing was weird and would continue to be, and he had to deal with it. He hoped the AI felt some discomfort on her end as well but knew she'd never admit to it even if she did.

Athena reported, "He called for a car. I intercepted it at one of the other companies' phones and told them that this is the vehicle that will respond."

Cia announced, "Rolling." The watchers had reported that their targets were either staying in or moving on foot, which suggested they'd seen the surveillance and they'd chosen not to betray the presence of Arlox's assistant. The van pulled up to the curb as their target walked out, accompanied by a burly looking man in a suit.

"Dammit," Jax muttered and turned away from the window since he wasn't exactly popular with the Intelligence Division. Cia ran around and slid open the van's side door, then grabbed at the travel bag Quentin carried. The escort snarled, "We'll keep that," and leaned into the vehicle to check for danger. All he saw was the back of Jax's head and Dr. Cray's smiling face. He seemed satisfied as he clambered in and sat in the row behind Juno. Their target followed and sat beside his protector.

Cia closed the side door, climbed in the front, and asked, "Hospital, correct?"

The escort grunted, "Yeah."

"Coming right up." Before she got the vehicle moving, she succumbed to a series of coughs.

"Here. I have a cough drop. Let me get it for you," Juno said brightly. Her hands dug into her bag and came out holding two small aerosol cans. She twisted and sprayed the contents of the first at the guard, and the other at Quentin. The bigger man struggled for an instant, then slumped as the knockout drug did its work. The one that had hit Arlox's assistant had a different effect, and his face turned languid as he breathed, "Whoa." Cia pulled away and headed for the hospital as slowly as she could reasonably drive.

Juno withdrew a syringe with a superfine needle and injected both the guard and Quentin in the side of their hand, where the rough skin wouldn't easily show the puncture, even to a trained observer. Neither reacted, and she nodded in satisfaction. "Memory blocker should be doing its work now. They'll have no recollection of the trip or the minutes leading up to getting into the van. Plus, Quentin's hallucinogens seem to be working pretty well." The thin man laughed, and she shook her head with a smile. "It's all you, Jax."

He climbed into the row right in front of Quentin to switch places with Juno and knelt on the seat to face him. There was no such thing as a truth serum, per se, but the hallucinogens they'd dosed their target with would put him in a highly suggestible state, enough that he should accept most of what they told him without questioning it. The memory blocker would only last reliably for about fifteen minutes, and Cia was doing her best to ensure that at the end of that time, they'd be outside the hospital. Jax growled in a deep, authoritative tone, "Quentin. Pay attention. Did you hear me? If you don't do your job better, I'll have to fire you. The Intelligence Director can't have incompetent people working for him."

Quentin's eyes snapped open. "Director Arlox. I'm sorry. I don't know what happened. Can you repeat the question?"

Jax shook his head in annoyance. "I asked you to brief me on our upcoming travel schedule."

The other man frowned. "But I don't have that information, sir. You never release those details until the day before a move. As far as I know, we're planning to stay here for a while." Jax wanted to ask where *here* was, but the less unexpected content he threw at the other man, the better the chances of getting something useful would be. He waved a hand and wondered for a moment what Quentin saw. *An office, maybe.* "Unimportant. Give me a full report on our current operations. Start with the hunter teams."

He nodded. "Yes, Director. Of course." His subservient tone was painful to hear. Apparently, Arlox treated those closest to him with the same disdain he spread over everyone else who interacted with him. "The ones sent after Reese failed. Our belief is the artificial intelligence gave him an edge of some kind, either physically or simply in awareness. The presence of Academy people defeated our trap at his destination, so clearly they knew it was coming."

Jax grunted. "How do you think they found out?"

The other man shrugged. "I'm not a technician, sir, but I

presume that they intercepted comm transmissions, or they had standing surveillance on the station in Inverness."

"Probably the latter. Continue." Didn't hurt to hide the fact that the agents they'd had on the ground that day had a vulnerability in their comms that Athena had been able to exploit.

"The ones on Maarsen and the girlfriend were unable to breach the castle grounds. The defenses have been significantly increased over the norm, and rebuffed them before they could gain access to the building. I'm sure it didn't help that it was daylight."

"Most likely wouldn't have mattered. They'll have locked that building down hard. We probably shouldn't try there again." Maybe that would ensure a level of safety to people at the Academy, anyway. "And the ones on his military supporters?"

The man's face twisted in confusion. "We weren't able to target them, sir, as you know. They are safe aboard ship for the moment."

He snarled, "That's not the kind of answer I want to hear. Why don't we have anyone on board?"

Quentin cringed. "We, we do, sir, but your orders were not to activate them until a guaranteed opportunity to take out the major presented itself. Has that changed?"

Bloody hell. "No, it hasn't. I was checking to make sure you had all the facts at your command, Quentin, and you do. Good job." The man beamed. Jax imagined that compliments from his boss were few and far between.

In his ear, Cia's voice whispered, "Eight minutes."

That left him only four to finish the interview before Juno would need access to their momentary captive to put the next part of their plan into play. "Very well. What about our plans for the Special Forces unit? We must eliminate everyone who can provide support to that bastard Reese."

"Proceeding as expected, sir, according to the last update." *Dammit. Why couldn't he give me something a little more than that?* Jax wracked his brain for another question to ask that wouldn't betray his lack of knowledge but failed to come up with one. So, he finished the way he'd been instructed. "Excellent, Quentin. Everything seems to be in order. It's good that you've devoted this time to take care of your family. You have my support. Stay alert." Jax traded places with Juno again, and the doctor used a larger injector with a bigger needle to shoot something into his calf, which required her to bend awkwardly but attractively over the backrest. She took her seat. "Check with your friend."

Jax didn't have to ask. Athena reported, "I detect no leakage from the nanoparticles. They appear to be operating as intended." The tiny tracking devices now moving through Quentin's bloodstream would remain inert for seventy-two hours, then would ping local networks with their location once a day for a fraction of a second. Anyone not listening for the signal at that precise moment would miss it.

Even better, they would leave his body over time as sweat and potentially tag other people who might be near him as well. The hope was that the spread would provide a pattern of Quentin's movements, those of Arlox's inner circle of subordinates, and eventually lead to hints about the director's plans or whereabouts. Like Jax had said when they'd come up with it, trying to use the assistant was a longshot, but it was the only one they had. He snickered. *There's that word again. Shot.*

Athena replied, "Keep practicing. Someday you might say something funny." Jax shook his head and stared out the window as they pulled up to the hospital's entrance. Cia scampered around and slid open the door, then touched the two men to wake them. "Geez, you guys must be tired. You fell asleep as soon as you got into the van. Didn't rest much last night?"

Both men looked bleary, but neither seemed overly concerned about it. Quentin nodded. "My parents are in the hospital. They might not make it."

Cia's impressive acting skills were on display as she expressed her sympathies and helped the two men out of the car. "Take care, and I hope everything turns out all right. If you need a ride somewhere, you know where to find me." She slid the door closed and patted the logo on the side. "It's been a pleasure serving you."

Jax thought, *Now it's your turn to serve us by leading us straight to your scumbag of a boss.*

CHAPTER EIGHT

Zavian Arlox was annoyed. He had spent most of the day that way, encountering a succession of aggravating situations as the hours passed. Meetings with pesky people, listening to irritating reports and answering vexing questions that his capable assistant Quentin would generally have handled. He'd sent the man off with his blessing, although part of him had wanted to remind his assistant that his presence wouldn't make a difference in whether his family members survived or not. That sort of emotional frailty was not a thing Arlox could identify with. Perhaps at one time in his life he might have understood it, but years of being the Alliance's primary spymaster had eliminated most traces of compassion from his personality. Now there was only duty: the need to protect his people and their way of life from the constant threats presented by the Coalition and the Confederacy.

He looked up from the work on his desk as his office door opened, prepared to dress down whoever dared to interrupt him. However, he'd lost track of time because the woman who strode in was his second in command, and they had a standing meeting at nine in the evening whenever they were in the same location. He pushed aside the tablet in front of him with a sigh. "Jasmine, grab us some drinks before you sit."

She was almost as tall as he was, a few inches shy of six feet, and had long brunette hair she wore straight in a curtain that fell to the middle of her back. That mane was the one imprecise thing about her. Her suit was sharp and exquisitely tailored. The skirt ended just below her knees, and the crisp white blouse was a perfect counterpoint to the gray jacket. Her boots were calf-high, polished black, and stylish. He studied her profile as she dropped a ball of ice into two tumblers and filled them each with a triple shot of whiskey. Her nose was a little too pointy for his taste, but it suited her face's strong lines. She was someone who had never relied on her looks but instead traded on the force of her personality and the keen spark of her intellect. Those were the factors that had drawn him when he selected her from among his top lieutenants to serve as his right hand when the last one failed him for a second time.

She slid a glass across the desk as she sat in the chair opposite him, crossed her legs, and adjusted the skirt. He asked, "Any crises?"

Jasmine's voice was dry, not quite sarcastic but seemingly always on the edge of it. "None that we didn't face this morning when we woke up." The comment made him think of how pleasant it might be to wake up with her by his side, but Arlox was never one to mix business with pleasure. *Too much chance of getting close to someone who could betray you.*

"Okay. Tell me about the Academy."

"The hunter teams got no further than we expected them to, but did provide a useful test of the building's external defenses. We believe there might be a blind spot in the back now, but can't be positive based on this limited trial. They may have moved people around inside rather than on the outer grounds, which could account for why we didn't see a response from that area to the incursion at the front. Or it could be that they're simply quite disciplined. But I would put my money on no human guards assigned to the rear courtyard. Surveillance, certainly. Perhaps traps, likely mechanical deterrents of some kind."

Arlox nodded with a slight frown. "But you think that would be the better choice for an assault if we needed to make one soon?"

"I do. If we sent in robotic cannon fodder to trigger the traps, and an attack wave right behind them, we might be able to get inside before their personnel could respond."

He tapped a finger on the tablet on the desk while thinking. "We would likely have to use some expendable soldiers as well, in case there were traps that were only set off by something particularly human. Electromagnetic fields, temperature, whatever." He waved a hand. "You know."

She sipped her drink, then carefully set it back on the round wooden coaster that protected the desk from its moisture. "I do. We have mechanicals programmed to emulate all those things, but you are correct, better not to take chances. We can requisition some from the local military base in England if it becomes necessary."

"Very good. Any sign of Reese?"

Jasmine shrugged. "None so far. We were forced to discontinue surveillance on the Academy after our attack since they were very much on the lookout. We've lost a few drones since then while trying to get a sense of the situation. I estimate it will still be several days or a week before their defenses lower enough that we'll be able to reinsert any significant oversight. But we've not seen any evidence of him in Inverness or Edinburgh after his arrival."

Arlox grunted an acknowledgment. "And the spaceport?"

"It's being protected too carefully for us to have surveillance there, either. The ship Reese used before isn't present, but we have no idea when it departed, if he was on it when it did, or where it went."

"No satellite recordings?" His voice held a note of surprise since the Intelligence Division had access to every surveillance device the Alliance possessed.

She shook her head. "Interestingly, our satellites over that area have gaps in their recordings."

Arlox slapped a palm down on the desk in frustration. "Damn you, Maarsen. You're a clever bugger." He sipped his drink and steadied his voice. "See that we get some of our technology into place. He'll find it far harder to crack our systems than the military's." The scorn in his tone indicated his opinion of the quality of the armed forces' resources.

She nodded. "Will do. In other news, Quentin called. His parents are recovering."

"Good. Everything seemed normal there?"

"Also interestingly, several of our operatives were

under surveillance during or around the time that Quentin was on Mars."

He scowled. "Could be something targeted at Quentin, could be random chance. In any case, see to it that he takes the standard roundabout on the way back. Make sure no one can follow him to us." The regular procedure involved a sort of shell game of ships and shuttles that would shake off anyone trying to follow. It added a good seventy-two hours to the travel time from any one place to another, but it had proven effective in the past, and there was no way in this time of heightened risk that they would abandon it. Still, four or more days without his assistant wasn't something to look forward to. He took another drink to ease the pain of that realization.

Jasmine shrugged. "Sometimes a coincidence is just a coincidence, but it doesn't hurt to be sure."

"We need to get that damned intelligence out of Reese's head. Otherwise, it will still be possible that someone could counter us. Is everything in place for our move against the Confederacy, the Snellar, and the Krastow?" The proper pronunciation of the alien species names required more effort than he was willing to give it.

"Proceeding as expected. The resources you moved into place on Ventralia are setting things up, and additional resources will be brought to bear over the next few days. We can't bring everyone in at once, or we risk them noticing and either taking offense or getting suspicious. But there is one small snag."

He sighed. "There always is. What is it?"

"They're demanding that you be present for the demonstration."

He rolled his eyes. "Of course they are. They like to jerk my chain and make me dance to their tune. Do you see any way to avoid it?"

She shook her head slowly while considering the question. "Not without potentially damaging the relationship."

Arlox nodded. "It's too close to the pivotal moment to risk such a thing. I'll be there, but force them to work for it. Get whatever luxuries or concessions you can out of them." It wasn't so much the actual things that were important, but the fact that his people would make the others pay for demanding his presence. *Proprieties have to be maintained.* He chuckled. "Do you have any good news at all?"

She grinned. "Absolutely. The whiskey is delicious." He laughed, and she continued, "But yes, I do. The plan to address the military side of Reese's support system is moving along nicely." Arlox leaned forward, interested. He had set up the plan's broad outlines but had then left it in her hands until she required his input again.

Jasmine continued, "We've identified a planet that's right on the border between the Confederacy and us, but close enough to the Coalition that it makes sense they would want it, too. The Confederacy currently owns it, but we're going to mess with their surveillance to allow the Coalition to move on them. We've explained that the Alliance is uninterested in the planet but wants to be sure the Confederacy doesn't keep it. It's an opportunity they won't be able to pass up."

He smiled. "Let me guess. Before the aliens can reinforce it, we're going to send in a team to take it."

She offered him a thin smile. "Exactly. We have the right people in place to put the right words in the proper ears to make recommending the move seem like a career maker. I have no question that the day after the attack, the *Cronus* will enter the system and deploy all its Special Forces teams down to the planet."

He gave a knowing nod. "And the trap?"

Jasmine shrugged. "We'll let the Confederacy in on the situation too late to stop the Alien Coalition, but in time to catch Stephenson's people on the planet. Battle will ensue, perhaps some mechanicals will go haywire, and Jackson Reese's people, the other two teams, and the wench that leads them all will be no more."

"We're covered?"

She nodded. "We have enough blackmail material on the guy who will be unwittingly speaking up on our behalf to initiate the action that he won't dare turn on us once we make him aware of it. And if he does, well, his shiny young girlfriend that his wife doesn't know about is one of ours. She can eliminate him and make it look natural."

Arlox leaned back and took a deep drink of his whiskey. "Well, I have to admit it sounds like things are moving in the right direction. After we wipe out everyone that bastard Reese can turn to for help, we're going to take him and carve that AI out of his head while he's still alive so he can fully appreciate the experience."

CHAPTER NINE

The *Grace* landed at the airfield two days after the operation against Arlox's assistant. They'd chosen the prudent move of looping around in such a way that they wouldn't appear to be coming from Mars, since someone was surely watching by now. The crew had spent the extra time aboard ship resting, relaxing, and doing a little light training. Even Trianna had joined in the social meals and had spoken a few words, although not specifically directed at Jax. *One day she's going to talk to me. I swear.*

Athena snorted. "No one would talk to you unless they had to, Jax."

Cruel. How can you be so cruel? The vans were waiting, and they were back at the Academy within thirty minutes of landing, arriving just after the dinner hour. They said their goodbyes, and Jax hugged Juno while the others wandered off to their destinations. "So, are we still on for tomorrow? You haven't thought better of it?"

She looked up at him with a grin. "No, I take my responsibilities as your pity date seriously."

He sighed and released her as she gently pushed away from him. As she walked off, he called, "You know, the way you said that is like I'm the one dating you out of pity."

She shot back, "But obviously no one would ever believe that could be possible, since I'm so clearly out of your league." His comm buzzed with a text message before he could yell out a witty counter, and he looked down to see an invitation from Stephenson to join her in the downstairs bar. He stopped at his room to drop off his travel bag, then headed down.

The place was busier than he would've expected for an early evening, with most of the tables and booths filled. The displays hung everywhere showed a sport he didn't recognize that looked like baseball but used a board instead of a bat. His superior officer was at the bar, receiving a drink from Coach. He slid in next to her. "One of the same for me, please." The dark-skinned man nodded, stroked his mustache once as if to reassure himself that it was as lush and beautiful as always, and bustled off to pour drinks for a trio that had wandered up to the bar. Jax greeted, "Hello, Major. Didn't think you could get away from the ship."

She gave a soft snort. "There's a big difference between taking a formal leave and spending a couple of days on R&R. Besides, with Arlox headed to Earth, I thought maybe my presence here would stir the pot a little."

Jax frowned. "He's coming here?"

She peered down at her comm. "He's probably on-planet by now. He has meetings with the muckety-mucks in the government."

He accepted his drink from the bartender and took a

deep pull on the draft IPA, then winced at the bitterness. "Damn, you're going for the potent stuff tonight. Everything okay?"

She laughed. "Everything's fine, within the boundaries of, you know, the universe. Can't get a drink like this on the *Cronus*."

"With good reason. Half the crew would be drunk half the time if you could."

"Only the weak ones."

Jax took another sip, which went down smoother. "So, how's Wasp working out?"

Stephenson grinned. "O'Leary is doing every bit as well as we knew she would. She's done a fine job of building rapport with the new team member, and I'm already looking for the best opportunity for her once you're back. She'll be one of the great ones."

"Like me, you mean."

She turned to him and lifted an eyebrow. "Did I say that? I don't think I did."

He shook his head sadly. "Why must every person in my life be so cruel? You're all a bunch of meanies."

They laughed together, and Stephenson said, "Seriously, she's keeping the team at every bit as high a level as it was with you in charge. You should be able to step right back in."

He nodded. "Of course, that assumes Arlox doesn't kill me before then. How much danger do you think my unit is in?"

She shrugged. "No more than on any other day. There's no way he'll get to them on the *Cronus*, and I don't see how he could while we're deployed, either. That essentially leaves when they're away from the ship on personal business, but that seems doubtful too."

"How's your aide?"

She chuckled and shook her head. "Striking terror into the hearts of anyone who wants a piece of my time. She's brilliant."

"Didn't choose Lyton, huh? Romantic tension too high?"

She laughed and slapped a palm on the bar. "Oh, please. Definitely not my type. I like them pretty."

"Yeah, me too."

"Things progressing between you and the doctor?"

"Slowly but surely."

She gave him a shrewd look. "So much so that you're considering not returning to the *Cronus*?"

He gave a small scowl at being so transparent. "The thought had crossed my mind. But how do *you* know that?"

She patted him on his arm. "You're not exactly as closed a book as you think you are, Jackson. But also, there's a certain allure to being here at the Academy. I considered leaving the military and staying here. It's only natural that you would, too. The lovely Dr. Cray certainly offers additional motivation."

He shrugged. "We're not there yet. I won't make any decisions in the immediate future. Speaking of the immediate future, know anything about your upcoming missions?" In truth, he missed the camaraderie of the Special Forces. His relationship with his Academy team, except for Cia and Juno, didn't have the same depth of connection as his SF comrades.

She nodded. "There's something in the works. I'm sure

of that much. I've received a quiet word here and there about a planet that the Confederacy holds on our border. Seems like one of the alien races, or maybe the Coalition as a whole, is taking a hard look at it."

"Which means the possibility exists that we'll go in to take it from whoever wins that conflict."

She shrugged and finished her beer, then set down the empty glass and signaled for another. "That does tend to be how it works. I can't imagine why we wouldn't."

Jax drained his as a second arrived for him as well and nodded his thanks to the bartender. "Sounds like a golden opportunity to mess with our people."

"Any deployment will be. I don't see any way we can predict when or if such a thing will happen unless we get another quiet word warning us ahead of time." She shrugged. "We'll have to operate with our eyes open, right?"

He nodded. "Seems reasonable to me. So, do you think you would ever come back here full-time?"

Stephenson laughed. "Maarsen asked me that earlier today. I'll tell you what I told him. When it feels right, I'll make that move. I can't foresee a situation where it doesn't happen, eventually. But for now, I still have people to take care of and things to accomplish."

"Did he try to talk you into it?"

She tilted her head toward the entrance. "You can ask him yourself."

Maarsen circled the bar to stand between them and called, "Coach, the usual, please." A tumbler of whiskey was in his hand moments later, and he suggested, "How about we move to a corner table where things are a little quieter?"

When they slid into their seats in the least populated part of the tavern, Jax asked, "How come you haven't convinced Major Stephenson to be here full-time yet, Professor?"

Maarsen chuckled. "It's not for lack of trying, believe me. I've told her she could write her ticket. It's that damnable streak of loyalty she has for the military and her subordinates. Deeply frustrating." They all laughed together.

She replied, "You mean it's frustrating because I'm loyal to people other than you."

He nodded. "Of course. The Academy and I are *obviously* the most important things in the universe."

Jax shook his head. "How did you wind up on the opposite side of Zavian Arlox?"

Maarsen leaned back in his chair and sighed. "That's a story. Once upon a time, I worked in government. He was part of a different department and already had his sights set on the Intelligence Division. We knew each other from interactions between our areas, and our similar intellectual approaches to problem-solving drew us together. We were very much alike in our dedication to the Alliance's future, but even then it was obvious that while I had some lines I considered uncrossable, Arlox had nothing of the sort. For him, the end was so important that it justified whatever needed to be done in its service." He sighed. "Finally, the inevitable happened, and I bumped up against something I wasn't willing to do. I wound up here because I knew I couldn't achieve any lasting change within the system and remain true to myself. He, of course, embraced the system and clawed his way up to a position of almost unmatched power."

Jax frowned. "If the government had the will, it could certainly pull him back."

Maarsen shrugged. "I would say that's an arguable point. By now, he probably has blackmail information on anyone who could harm him. If he doesn't, whoever isn't under his thumb should consider taking out a large life insurance policy."

Stephenson tapped a finger on the table. "That's why I feel the need to stay inside, at least for the moment. Once all internal resistance is gone, who knows what Arlox and those like him in the government might get up to?"

Jax asked, "Do you think he's going to make a move on my Special Forces team?" He summarized the conversation he and Stephenson had been having, and the major added a point or two of clarification.

The Professor nodded. "I'm positive he will. Impossible to know when, but he'll see them as a threat like he does the rest of us."

Jax frowned. "Maybe I should bring the Academy team along on their missions for a while. Provide a little extra support."

The others both shook their heads. Stephenson replied, "No way we can integrate civilians into our operation."

Maarsen added, "That's not what they signed up for when they agreed to work with the Academy. No, our tasks are different. This is one of those moments where you're going to have to choose whether you stick with us or go back to your team, I'm afraid. I will say that I think your efforts can achieve more here than they would there."

Stephenson agreed. "Wasp has your team under control. There's not much you could add right now. If the trap does show up and it's small enough that your influence would've made a difference, chances are we'll come through it okay, anyway. If it's big enough that you couldn't change the outcome, then there's no point putting you and the Academy's people in danger. So, no."

Jax sighed. "It was a dumb idea. Of course, I'll stay here. Maybe we can take him out before he has a chance to do anything else."

Stephenson nodded and lifted her glass. "To ridding the universe of one particular scumbag, as soon as possible." He and the Professor clinked their glasses and muttered cheers, but without much positivity.

Maarsen set his glass down and stared Jax in the eyes. "So, Jackson, tell me about your last mission again. Don't leave anything out. Let's get started on figuring out how to bring the good Zavian down right now."

CHAPTER TEN

Jax collapsed onto a large boulder at the top of the mountain and sighed. "This, right here, this is the life."

Juno plopped down next to him and shrugged off her backpack, then pulled out a water bottle and took a long drink. "You don't do anything by half-measures, do you? You had to pick the biggest mountain on the entire island for our hike."

He'd convinced Juno to give up a whole day for recreation, with the Professor's blessing, of course. A small boat had delivered them to the Isle of Skye, where they'd ducked into a hiking store and purchased the extra stuff necessary for the climb. Most of their standard gear was sufficiently hardy, like boots and the Academy's uniforms, but neither had owned walking sticks or had the proper floppy hats to protect their heads and faces from the blazing sun above. While the black fabric of their trousers and shirts had been too warm at the base, they were just right by the midpoint of their climb.

The hike up the mountain had taken three hours along

a rough trail of switchbacks, small rock falls to navigate, and thick bunches of trees that occasionally turned daytime into twilight. They'd climbed leisurely, neither of them in any hurry, focused on enjoying their day together and sharing random information from their lives. Jax was cognizant that this was a respite, a brief moment in time between dangerous happenings. He'd been in the situation often enough to learn to embrace what joy he could find in those interludes enthusiastically.

Juno hadn't given any clues about whether she had previously faced the sorts of dangers she now found herself in. Still, she seemed lighter, happier, and more relaxed than he'd seen her at any time other than during their trip to her favorite nightclub.

Jax asked, "Anything to eat in there?"

"I told you that only bringing ration bars was a poor decision." She dug inside and pulled out a pouch of trail mix for each of them. He accepted it gratefully and tore it open with his teeth and a growl. She laughed. "Really, the barbarian thing isn't as appealing as you seem to think it is."

Jax grinned. "Me, Jax. Me man. Woman like man. *Tough* man."

Juno rolled her eyes. "Maybe I should take Ethan up on his suggestion to find someone whose brainpower is greater than their physical power."

He countered, "Hey, how many other people in your dating pool have a cutting-edge artificial intelligence lodged in their brain? Not a large number, I'd imagine. I've got it all, baby." He gave a small bodybuilder's flex with his arms, and she laughed again.

"You've got something all right, Jackson Reese. I'm not sure it's 'all' of anything, though."

He frowned. "That didn't make sense."

She laid back on the rock and wriggled her shoulders to get comfortable. "I know. I think I'm getting dumber from prolonged exposure to you."

He laughed and reclined beside her, angling himself so his temple touched hers. "You'll find that it's lovely, almost blissful, to let all that brainpower go and just exist."

"So you're a Buddhist now, is that it?"

He shrugged. "By and large, Special Forces is the religion of everyone who belongs to it. But if forced to decide on a different affiliation, a standard dollop of monotheism with a side dish of Buddhism would fit."

Juno sounded theatrically impressed. "Those are mighty big words. Do you know what they mean, or did you read them on the back of a cereal box?"

He closed his eyes and basked in the early afternoon sunlight on his face. "I believe the universe is too complicated to be truly random. Somewhere there's a consciousness, a being, a plan, a reason, whatever you want to call it. I tend to think of it as an intellect, which is close enough to the typical idea of a deity that it works out. But I also believe we should try to enjoy what we can when we can. Of course, goals and objectives and such are vitally important. But one doesn't have to sacrifice their entire life to them. We need to find a way to live life in the cracks and crevices of our obligations."

"That's pretty deep, for a meathead."

He laughed. "I think the term you're going for is jarhead. It's not very nice, and I'm also not a Marine." He tilted his head to look at her. "How about you? What's your philosophy on life?"

"Complicated, I'd say."

When she didn't continue, Jax said, "Okay, you've said that. Now, how about saying a little more? Or do you think I'm not smart enough to understand it?"

She smiled. "No, just putting my thoughts in order. I've always wanted to be a doctor. I think that desire was originally rooted in the religious ideal of taking care of one's community, being good to others, being a shepherd to a flock in need. You know the drill."

"I can see that. A lot of folks in the military feel the same way."

She nodded. "But at some point, I realized the whole outward-facing self-sacrifice narrative could only take me so far. Psychology through the ages has proven that we have an intrinsic need for success, for self-actualization as the scientists say. For me, serving others wasn't the right route to that. Or perhaps it's fairer to say that it couldn't get me all the way there. Maybe it would rise to that level for a priest or a missionary. I don't have that sort of purity."

Jax quipped, "Are you coming on to me? Because you don't have to be subtle. You can tell me your desire, and it can happen right here. There's no one around."

She laughed. "Shut up, you. I have no doubt there's a drone nearby and keeping an eye on us, courtesy of the Academy."

Jax waved up into the sky. "Hi, Academy people. Juno doesn't want you to see her enjoying herself. Go away."

She backhanded him in the stomach with a snort. "Anyway, that's why I moved out of practicing medicine as my main job and into research. It brings something out in me that I haven't been able to find anywhere else. So, to sum it all up, I started with the best of intentions, religion, community, and so forth, but eventually turned to the dark side of science and knowledge acquisition."

Jax shook his head. "Those distinctions don't matter. You can be both, regardless of what anyone else says. And I guess that comes back to the core of my philosophy if I have one. We all make our choices, then we all live with them. Anyone suggesting otherwise is someone who isn't willing to accept responsibility for themselves."

Juno shrugged. "It's not the worst theory I've heard. That doesn't mean I fully agree with you, though. It's a little one-size-fits-all for me."

"Well, give it time. You might eventually reach the state of enlightenment that I've achieved."

"Yeah, sure, that's it." She stretched. "It'll be faster going back, right?"

Jax had been surprised at her lack of experience with hiking, given how healthy and generally physically adept she was. He shook his head. "Slower, actually. All those places that were solid footholds on the way up can prove treacherous on the way down, so we have to be more careful. Plus, if you thought your thighs hurt from the ascent, you're going to hate the descent." In truth, his legs were reminding him that he'd spent too little time in the gym of late.

She sat up and smacked her thighs. "Well, I'm starving, and since the reward for this is something much nicer than trail mix and ration bars, I say we get moving."

The climb down had proved unproblematic except for a couple of places where one or the other of them fell and slid a short distance. In each case, they came up laughing. They reached the bottom and headed into Portree on rented scooters. He would've preferred a motorcycle, but the small fishing village turned tourist destination didn't have anything of the sort. What it did offer was brightly painted buildings a stone's throw from the water's edge, uncrowded streets with more pedestrians than vehicles, and a general atmosphere of quiet relaxation.

Pleasure boats filled the marina at one end of town, and at the other end, a businesslike dock had berths for fishing vessels to bring in their cargo at the end of the day. The village did a brisk tourist trade, as evidenced by the fact that public showers and changing rooms were available for those who didn't plan to rent a room. He'd resisted suggesting to Juno that they conserve resources by showering together, but only just. As the water cascaded over him, he thought about their relationship. *I'm sure I'm not misjudging her interest level or the serious tension between us.*

Athena, who had agreed to be quiet for the day when he was with Juno, replied, "Or it's been a long time for you, and you see the things you want to see."

Hush. I've dated enough people to be confident that she's interested. And before you say it, I don't know why either, I'm just happy that she is.

The AI made a sound like a long-suffering sigh. "I guess I have to give you that much credit. For whatever delusional reason she might possess, Dr. Cray does seem to be entranced by your charms."

He laughed. *Charms. I don't think that's a word I would associate with me. It sounds too posh.*

Athena replied, "Maybe I'm a positive influence on you. Perhaps our conversations are increasing your IQ very slowly over time." She paused with perfect comedic timing to let him appreciate the idea that he was getting smarter, then added, "That explains it. Dr. Cray will write a paper about you for some journal to make herself famous. That explains everything."

He turned off the water and grabbed a towel. "Shut it, you." Some things needed to be said out loud.

He dressed in the finer clothes that he'd stored in a locker at the facility during their climb: polished shoes, dark trousers, and a light gray cable-knit sweater. He threw his hiking outfit in his pack and headed out to meet Juno. He spent a few minutes watching the waves, listening to the seagulls complaining overhead, and enjoying the breeze coming in off the water. From behind him, Juno commented, "Ooh, nice sweater. Is it soft?" He turned, and the hand she'd stretched out to touch his arm landed on his chest instead.

He raised an eyebrow. "What do you think?"

She blushed a little and let the hand fall. "I think we need to get to dinner. I'm famished." She had on an outfit entirely dissimilar to anything he'd ever seen her wear. Tall brown suede boots reached up to right below her knees, and the darker brown skirt that ended above them swirled and moved with each step she took. She wore a black tank top with a maroon man's dress shirt atop it, unbuttoned most of the way. Her makeup was simple, a little highlight on the eyes, cheeks, and lips, and her hair was pulled back in a ponytail. She looked entirely appropriate for the occasion and completely beautiful. He managed to choke out, "You're gorgeous. I mean, your outfit looks great." He thought about it for a second and shook his head. "No, what I mean is you are stunning." He leaned over and kissed her lips softly, then leaned back and grinned. "Now, how about some food?"

He had chosen a restaurant called Scorrybreac, located in a converted house a couple of streets back from the water. He'd requested an out-of-the-way table, which turned out to be in what was probably a butler's pantry at one point but was now lavishly decorated with fabrics and paintings on the walls. Sconces at the corners held soft lights that bounced off the ceiling, and the space held only a single table, set for two. He chuckled as they entered. "Okay, so I didn't specifically ask them to seat us by ourselves, for the record."

She laughed as she took the chair being held out for her by the dark-suited maître d'. "Sure, Jax. Sure."

Jax looked up at the other man. "Little help here?"

The maître d' shook his head with a smile. "I learned long ago that one never argues with a guest."

He left before Jax could press him further. The meal was a tasting menu, starting with a delicate cream cheese and salmon combination on fresh, toasted bread. Two different kinds of fish followed and were themselves followed by a hunk of venison that was as delicious as any meat he'd ever tasted. An array of smaller bites of vegetables and fruit complemented each course. They chatted amiably through the meal and shared a bottle of light red wine that paired better with the deer than the fish, but was nonetheless perfect for the evening. The next-to-last taste was a lemon ice as a palate cleanser, then coffee arrived, along with pistachio cake covered with fresh strawberries.

Despite all the variety, there was only enough food to leave them content but not stuffed. He suggested, "How about a walk down the main street before we head back?"

Juno smiled and nodded, and they headed outside. She linked her arm in his as they sauntered along the sidewalk. "So, what does your future hold?"

Jax sighed. "A lot of conflict in the near term, I would say."

"And after that?"

He shrugged. "I always figured I would wind up at a training base teaching recruits. But after talking it over with my ever so brilliant superior officer, I think I can do more good by working with the Academy for a while instead."

She chuckled. "Community and shepherding into your old age?"

He stared out at the waves. "No, I'm not trying to buy my way into some deity's good graces. It's just that when I joined the Special Forces, I believed in that mission. I still believe, but being at the Academy has helped me realize I can be more, I can do more, than what's possible for a soldier. I've never wanted to rise into the top command ranks, so taking a different path seems like the best option. Both for my satisfaction, and for my ability to make the universe a little better." He looked down at her. "How about you?"

She gave a small smile. "I love Scotland, I love what I do, and there's nowhere I can think of where I would have the opportunity to learn and do such a variety of things. I'll be staying at the castle for the foreseeable future."

Jax grinned. "Good. Maybe I'll see you around then." They both laughed. Reluctantly, Jax observed, "If we're going to get back without crashing the boat, we probably need to leave soon. It's supposed to get cloudier as the night wears on."

Juno stopped and turned to him, then stood on her tiptoes to plant a long kiss on his mouth. "I rented us a room at a bed-and-breakfast a block over. Work can wait. Come along, Neanderthal."

CHAPTER ELEVEN

The next several days passed in a haze of normalcy as they all waited for the information to get back to them from the bugs in the assistant's bloodstream. The tiny devices were pinging as intended, but they had yet to reach an aggregate amount of data sufficient to point in a useful direction. When he asked, everyone told him to have faith that it would work out, and he chose to believe them. He spent every free moment he could with Juno and found that things kept getting better. Even Athena had quit suggesting the relationship wasn't a real thing, which he took as a good sign.

He'd arranged to meet Harrington, the Academy's weapons master, to continue working on training his prosthetics. Knowing that events were moving toward a climax, he pushed himself as hard as he could and spent a large part of his free hours doing everything from juggling to knife throwing to skipping rope in order to improve the coordination and speed of his artificial limbs. Whenever he juggled, he thought back to his first "real" class at the Academy. It seemed like a long time had passed since then, although in the grand scheme of things it truly hadn't.

He strode into the room where he'd welcomed Kenton Marshall to the Academy to find the weapons master waiting for him. The other man said, "Hello, Jax. Ready for some more abuse, then?"

Jax laughed. "Only if you're good enough to get them past me."

Harrington grinned. "I feel confident I'll be up to the task yet again."

Jax shook his head and strode to the opposite side of the room from where his partner stood in front of the weapons cabinets. On a narrow table beside him rested several objects, ranging from as small as a ping-pong ball to as large as a basketball. During their first session, the man had used his hands to throw them at Jax and challenged him to catch them with quick movements. Later, he had added tools to the mix, including a slingshot and a hydraulic launcher that currently stood to his left. He had also changed from simply throwing the balls for him to catch to randomly aiming them at his body, which forced Jax to defend himself. It seemed as if he understood the training's ultimate goal and took pleasure in helping Jax reach it. *As a good teacher should.*

Athena drawled, "Or he simply enjoys trying to hurt you."

There's a lot of that going around. Jax nodded. "Have at it."

The other man's arms were a blur as he hurled the smallest objects, which were far heavier than they looked and hurt a lot if they struck anyplace even remotely tender. Jax did his best to catch them and felt the slight tremors in his limbs as Athena performed her magic to speed him up or slightly adjust the trajectory of his motions. Initially, he had found himself resisting her efforts. It took him a while to realize he was, and longer to overcome his resistance to sharing control of his body with his passenger. But ultimately she proved right: they were much greater than the sum of their parts when he didn't get in the way of their partnership.

Without warning, the weapons master slammed one of the basketball-sized objects into the hydraulic launcher, and it shot out at Jax's face. He'd learned early not to try to catch those, and instead leaned to his right and brought that arm around to deflect it over his left shoulder. Another followed instantly, forcing him to sway in the other direction. The weapons master stopped after a dozen minutes or so. "I think you're ready."

He turned to the cabinet behind him and pulled out four matching knives, each of them dulled for training purposes but still hard enough to hurt if they hit. He threw them in quick succession to Jax, who caught and returned them in a single motion, juggling the weapons with the other man. They spun and tumbled through the air. Then the weapons master added a fifth. When they had the pattern going, and Jax thought he had it all figured out, his partner leaned to his side and shouldered the launcher, which fired a ball that Jax hadn't known was loaded. He couldn't think, only react. He managed to slap it aside without breaking the pattern, the speed of his newly replaced arm faster than ever. Harrington caught the knives on the return and set them aside. "Satisfied?"

"I am." *Athena, how about you?*

"We can do better, but gains from here on out will be minor. We're at least ninety percent capable with the new limbs."

Jax nodded. "Thanks for the training. I appreciate it." He strode forward and shook the other man's hand.

"It's what I'm here for. Any time."

Jax headed back to his room to shower, then started along the path that would take him to meet Juno for lunch. He only made it halfway before Athena informed him, "We finally have real information. Professor Maarsen will be calling a meeting in moments." Sure enough, the summons came as she finished speaking. He sent his apologies and directed his steps toward the basement training room and the conference area that lay behind it. When he got there, Maarsen stood at the far end of the room, the Academy quartermaster Hellene was seated at the table, and Stephenson was present on a display on the left wall. That view split as Athena took over half of it to show her avatar. As Jax took his seat, Harrington wandered in. He grinned. "Jax, long time no see."

Jax nodded as Maarsen said, "Our last mission has finally borne fruit." He gestured at the monitor behind him, and it came to life, showing a schematic of several systems. One was their solar system, and a cluster of brightly colored dots was located on Earth, centered around Tokyo. "That'll be Arlox and his closest people, meeting with the UCCA government at its headquarters."

The quartermaster asked, "Any way we can use that to our advantage?" Jax, Maarsen, and Stephenson all shook their heads. The Professor replied, "It's too obvious an opportunity. He'll have his defenses up against any action on our part. While it seems like a great chance, in truth, it's probably our least viable alternative unless someone here has an army hiding in their pocket."

He indicated the remaining two systems. One had only a few markers, while the other seemed to be a main transit point. Lines entered it from all angles and exited it in as many directions. It looked vaguely like a child's line drawing of the sun. He ordered, "Enlarge B, please." The more densely marked of the two filled the screen. "This is the Stryphus system. It's located in the closest third of the Alien Coalition's territory relative to our border. What's strange is that our previous surveys of the area, admittedly from long ago, indicated there's no life there to speak of. The planets are too far from the star to meet the needs of any species we've ever encountered. Some scientists believe the dying sun will eventually become so unstable that the planets may pull away from it and wander off to be captured by other systems." The pleasure in his voice while relating that information spoke to his overall love of teaching and sharing knowledge.

The weapons master asked, "Major Stephenson, is there a way for you to take a look at it?"

She scowled and shook her head. "Any resources I pulled would be recorded by the *Cronus*, which by now Arlox has doubtless compromised either electronically or with human knowledge." She looked entirely annoyed at that circumstance as if the fact that the Intelligence Director was good at his job was a personal affront. "So, unless we want them to know what we're up to, I can't do a damned thing."

Jax shrugged. "Guess we gotta do it the old-fashioned way and send some actual eyeballs in."

The quartermaster asked, "How about a drone?"

Maarsen tapped his chin with one long finger as he took his seat at the head of the table. "That seems like a reasonable possibility. It will take a little while to get it together, but it would be the safest route."

Jax shook his head. "I don't think so. From here on out, we have to assume that things could rocket to full speed at any moment. That means time will always be working against us. It makes the most sense to have me and my team go and see what's up so that if action is required, we can get to it right away."

The weapons master asked, "Do you have a plan?"

Jax shook his head. "No, but I'm good at improvisation." The others laughed, and he continued, "Seriously though, we load up the *Grace* with every piece of gear she can hold to give us maximum flexibility, then we go and react to what we see. We can always pull back or call in reinforcements if we need to, but this way if an opportunity presents itself, we're already in place and able to act."

Maarsen shook his head. "I don't like it, but that could be my conservative streak talking. Does anyone else have an argument to offer for or against?"

Stephenson offered, "It's a sound strategy, and it's more or less what Jax is best at. The question is whether the rest of the team is capable of handling it."

Jax shrugged. "They've risen to every challenge so far. I have no doubt they will again. I think they should be fully informed of the danger so that if anyone wants to step aside, they can. Maybe if that happens, we can meet up with some people from the *Cronus* who coincidentally decide it's a good time to take leave."

Stephenson said, "Again, anything involving us carries a serious risk of discovery. I wouldn't want to do it unless it was essential."

"I believe they'll all be on board with the plan. But they should have a choice."

Maarsen agreed, "Okay, you can ask them. But I won't authorize Dr. Cray to join you on this particular mission. She's too valuable to what we do here."

There were murmurs of assent from around the table, and Jax was secretly in full agreement. "Then you can be the one to tell her, Professor. I'm willing to brave some dangers, but not that one."

The other man grinned. "It won't be the first time I've frustrated her. Also, we should be sure to pull whatever data we can from Athena before you go, in case something goes terribly wrong."

What a gentle way to describe our demise, Professor. On the screen, Athena's avatar nodded decisively. "Of course. We will need to ensure that we fully update the *Grace* with all the latest information the Academy has, plus the required technology to continue tracking the nanoparticles."

Maarsen nodded. "It's done then. We'll get the ship ready as fast as we can, then you and whichever members of your team want to go along will head out. Hellene and Harrington, it will be up to you to ensure that the new surveillance Arlox and his people have put in place around the castle and the airfield is defeated. Once the *Grace* jumps, we should be safe from them knowing where the team is headed. We probably can't hide their departure, but maybe we can keep them from noticing until the ship's already out of reach." He locked eyes with Jax. "Are you sure this is how you want to handle this?"

Jax nodded. "Positive. It's time to move into the final round with this jerk."

Athena added, "And it's a fight we're going to win by knockout. Count on it."

CHAPTER TWELVE

As expected, every member of his Academy team agreed to participate in the mission, even Trianna. The next morning found them all aboard the *Grace*, collectively overseeing the loading of a much bigger set of cargo supplies than they'd carried on his previous missions. It took all of them working together to get the crates arranged and strapped to the hardpoints in the floor while the pilots prepped the ship, and there was a sense of seriousness in the operation that was greater than any he'd felt with this group. *It's good that they recognize the danger. I wish I didn't have to ask them to risk it.*

He slapped the button to raise the cargo bay door, then ran forward to check on their timetable. Cia was in the left-hand seat as always, and her quiet copilot was in the right. He asked, "Everything proceeding as planned?"

Cia nodded. "Hellene tells us that they've chased off the human surveillance watching the spaceport and taken out any drones for a five-mile radius around it. There's not much new that we can do about satellites, but I've got a little something in mind that should help with the secrecy of our operation."

Jax put a hand on his chest in feigned shock. "You're telling me you made plans without running them by me, the rightful commander of this mission?"

She snorted. "Things involving the *Grace* are my concern, not yours. So how about you head to the back and think about the limitations of your power, you dictator wannabe?"

He sniffed sadly. "You wound me, flygirl."

"Whatever, jerkwad. Get. We're lifting off in less than a minute." She flipped on the ship's intercom and made the same announcement. He headed for his quarters with a grin, wanting to spend some quiet time thinking through the various hazards that might lie in the future. Jax was a firm believer in visualization, and there was no greater reassurance than entering a difficult situation and knowing what to do because he'd already lived it mentally. While there were too many variables for him to figure out all the possibilities, the more things he ran through the process ahead of time, the better off his team would be in the long run.

He sealed himself into his bunk with his eyes closed and let his mind wander through the paths leading forward from the current moment. It wasn't quite meditation, but it was as close to it as he was likely to get while on active duty. A smile grew as he remembered the mountaintop with Juno, and it widened at the thought of the remainder of that date.

Athena chided him, "Focus, Jax. I don't want to die

because you're busy acting like a hormonal, lovestruck teenage boy."

He shook his head. *You're jealous. Maybe someday you'll meet another nice AI, and you'll understand.*

"You barely have enough brainpower in here to support me. There's no way a second could fit."

He let his mind wander, and it seemed like only moments before the all-clear sounded. He hit the galley for a snack, passed some small talk with the crew, then returned to his cabin and stayed there until they landed on Mars. Visiting the Rearden estate had been part of the plan from the beginning since they needed to pick up some equipment they couldn't get anywhere else. Plus, Cia wanted to secure reloads for the weapon added to the *Grace* during a previous visit. That was probably the only reason she'd gone along with the idea of being in proximity to her relatives when it came right down to it.

When the rear cargo door opened, he wasn't surprised to see Standring waiting there in all his tall, thin perfection. The family butler and overseer of the Rearden estate was in the same black uniform as always, but his normally stern visage softened with a smile at the sight of first Cia, then Jax. He strode forward and shook hands with the other man. "Standring, good to see you again."

The butler lifted an eyebrow. "And in much better shape than last time you visited, Captain Reese."

Jax laughed. The previous time he'd been on the planet, he'd arrived inside a cargo container, barely alive. "That's the understatement of the year. How have you been? How's the family?"

Standring laced his fingers behind his back. "I am well,

and the family is the same as ever. Although, as you can see, some things have changed." He gestured to the side, and Jax followed the motion to see that Anders Rearden, Cia's father, had come out to the family's private landing pad to greet her.

Jax grunted in surprise. "That's a shocker. I wouldn't expect him to be here unless he was the one traveling."

The other man nodded. "It is, in fact, the first time he has greeted an arriving ship in person."

"Then I guess it's only appropriate that I go and offer my respects. There's nothing critical involved with his presence, is there?"

"Even if there were, Captain, it wouldn't be my place to say." His tone was light enough that Jax took it to mean there was no particular concern.

He clapped the butler's shoulder. "You're a good man, Standring. Will you coordinate getting the stuff loaded with the crew?"

"Of course." He turned to walk toward the others, who had gathered outside the ship and were awaiting instruction.

Jax wandered slowly over to the two Reardens and made sure both saw him coming so he didn't interrupt anything delicate. The older man was the first to speak. "Jackson, good to see you again. Decided to take a more ordinary means of transit this time, eh?"

Jax laughed and spread his hands. "As your daughter likes to say, I can on rare occasions be overly dramatic. But I try not to make a habit of it."

Cia snorted. "If by that you mean spending at least an

hour a day acting like a normal human, or as close as you can get to normal, then that's true." She shook her head and turned to her father. "Honestly, the phrase 'drama queen' was made for this one."

The older man laughed. "I remember you saying that about each of your brothers at least once, and several more times about your sister."

She nodded. "Yeah, but I hadn't met *him* yet. Compared to him, they're strictly amateurs."

Jax shook his head. "The level of abuse I get from these people is enough to make me want to go back to the Special Forces. Enemies shooting at me on a regular basis is less dangerous than this, psychologically speaking anyway."

Cia injected a note of baby talk into her voice. "Aww, is Jackson sad? Did the smart people's insults hurt his little feelings?"

He sighed, the other two laughed, and the conversation turned. Anders became serious. "Are you sure this mission is worth the risk?"

Jax looked at Cia. "You told him?"

She shook her head. "He figured part of it out by himself, based on what I requested. Given that our cargo bay is open and the ship is stuffed to the rafters, we're clearly heading out for something serious."

He nodded. "Fair enough. Yes, sir, I'm sure this is the right way to go. Everyone here is a volunteer, and I'll do my best not to put them at any excessive risk. But the issues at hand are too big, and the danger we're all in already too high, to delay decisive action any longer."

The other man nodded. "I've been in similar situations in the boardroom rather than the battlefield, and I understand where you're coming from. I hope the materials we provided help. Know that you can always come back here if you need to. Even other governments would think twice before ticking off a business as large as ours, especially given our extensive connections to the UCCA."

Jax laughed. "Hell, I'm counting on it. Once we're wanted criminals throughout the universe, I figured the whole group would move in with you. The house certainly has the space, and we'll promise not to be too much of a burden. I'll volunteer Marshall and Sirenno as chaperones for your kids."

Anders barked a short laugh. "In that circumstance, we would find a way to make it work." He turned to Cia. "I've said this to you before, but I'll say it again. I think you should consider coming to work with us, at least part-time. You can balance it with the activities you undertake for the Academy. It would be good for you, and good for us. We might even agree to put Jackson on the payroll as your copilot if you negotiated hard enough."

She rolled her eyes. "Go into business with this guy? Haven't you heard anything I've been saying? I'm hoping to leave him marooned on a planet in some uncharted system halfway across the galaxy so I don't have to deal with him anymore." Her tone softened, and she touched her father's arm. "I hear you. I'll think about it, *really* think about it. Truth is, I sort of miss being a part of all this. But there's no way I'll take orders from my siblings, even indirectly. So you better figure that if I come back, you'll need to create an independent division of some kind for me with its own resources and mandate." She paused for a second, then flashed a wide grin. "Or simply disinherit all of them and put me in charge of everything. That would work, too."

Anders groaned and shook his head. "I value my life too much to do such a thing. They've all grown up to be appropriately vicious businesspeople. In any case, I think your crew has finished loading."

Jax turned and saw that he was correct. "That's our cue, I guess. Better get inside. Always good to see you, sir."

The older man nodded once. "And you, Captain Reese. Be safe." He didn't say it out loud, but Jax understood the next part of his message, regardless. *And keep your crew, especially my daughter, safe.*

"Count on it, sir. You have my word." He turned and jogged toward the tail of the ship, where he did a little yelling and pointing to make sure everything was properly secured in place.

Jax didn't see Cia's return, only knew she was back when a terse "Prepare for liftoff," came over the intercom. He returned to his cabin, but this time flicked on the display to watch the view from the ship's nose camera. The *Grace* lifted off from the opened dome as usual but didn't climb toward space. Instead, she flew through the atmosphere and spent about forty-five minutes in the air before descending into the largest civilian spaceport facility he'd ever visited.

Once they landed, a tow truck dragged them into a nearby hangar, itself also larger than Jax had ever seen. When they stopped moving, Cia called for everyone to gather in the galley. "My father and I worked up this plan to make our departure a little less visible. I ran it by the Professor, and he agreed. I haven't mentioned it before now, well, mainly because I didn't feel like it." The others laughed. "It was time Jax got a taste of his own medicine, damn secretive bastard." There were cheers, and Verrand threw a wadded-up napkin she found on the table at him.

The pilot continued, "Right now, people who look a little like us and will pretend to be us are on the way to a nearby hotel, where my family's business booked rooms in our names. I made a call more or less in the open when we landed to let the company know the ship required some repairs and it would be a couple of days before we were able to leave. That, of course, is a lie. After an hour or two of preparation, we'll blast out of here and get on with our mission. What I need from you is this."

She went on to explain what she needed the crew to do. It involved loading the ammunition into the ship's weapon, uncrating certain supplies so they'd be readily available during their trip, and for a few of them, heading out to assist in disguising the ship. Jax was one of the latter, and he descended the cargo ramp beside Cia and Kimmel. The pilot had a tablet in her hand. She explained, "This is linked up to the ship's computers. I like to watch this from the outside whenever I can."

She tapped buttons on the tablet, and hull panels slid and rotated into new positions that altered the ship's lines dramatically enough that a scan wouldn't be able to identify it as the *Grace*. The short wings angled backward, which changed the ship's width, and sections of the top hull rose and shifted inward to make tall upside-down V-shapes, taking what had been flat and transforming it into a tall spine. The flat cover that hid the weapons system also rose and changed to fit into the arrangement. He shook his head at the ship's sophistication, and the creativity Cia had put into its design and upgrades.

The color scheme switched from the beautiful metallic sheen it had worn to a mottled, beat-up look that was more reminiscent of the *Jigsaw* than of the amazing craft Cia took such pride in. The panel with the grace note on the front blanked for a moment before a new image appeared, a line art cleaver with crimson blood dripping from the blade. When the activity was complete, Kimmel strode over and gestured to the hangar crew members, who immediately bustled forward to attach a pair of pods to the underside of each wing, further disguising the ship. Jax asked, "What are those?"

She grinned. "*Those* are secret, that's what those are." She laughed at his scowl. "Okay, I'll tell you what one of them is. It's the sensing suite we need to detect the nanoparticles. It made more sense to package it up and connect it this way than to try to modify the ship's sensors and code."

Athena added, "I would have told you, but Cia wanted it to be a secret."

Traitor. "And the other three?"

The pilot grinned. "A girl has to keep her secrets. Both me and my new ship, *Occam's Cleaver.*"

He rolled his eyes. "Really?"

She laughed. "Don't look at me. The Professor came up with that one."

Jax threw up his hands in defeat. "Okay, I give up."

Cia patted him on the shoulder and said in a soothing voice, "There, there. Soon you'll be back in charge, and the world will seem right again. But for now, since I'm still the commanding officer for the next twenty minutes or so, get your ass on the ship, soldier. We have a mission to begin."

CHAPTER THIRTEEN

They reached their destination in three jumps although they could've crossed the distance in fewer. Despite departing Mars under a fictitious name and with an altered ship body and drive signature, Jax had opted to take a less direct route that extended the trip by almost a full day. During the downtime, they continued to analyze the data they had on their enemies' movements and added two more sets of pings to it. The concentration of dots in the system they were headed toward increased each time, making it clear that they were correct to consider it important.

When Cia announced they were a minute from the end of the jump, Jax strolled to the pilot's compartment and took a position between the two chairs, one hand on the back of each. She counted down, and real space popped into view when she reached zero. An asteroid field surrounded the system, and they'd decided to jump in behind that barrier. It would put them a reasonable distance away from the clustered nanoparticle dots and lessen the likelihood of detection upon arrival.

She slowed the ship and guided it toward one of the asteroids while adjusting speed and trajectory so the *Cleaver* moved with the huge rock, ensuring it would hide her from the inside of the ring. She lifted a fist, and Trianna bumped it with hers. The copilot stated, "Excellent piloting."

Cia replied, "No biggie. I think we probably snuck in without being noticed. Time to put our passengers to work." She tapped the control panel to her left, and a display Jax hadn't seen before appeared. She pressed a fingertip against the largest virtual button, and a camera activated to show a wing pod opening. Within were four small drones hanging from hardpoints. She ejected two of them and told Trianna, "You have the second."

"Yep. I'll go low."

Cia nodded and manipulated the panel's controls to bring the drone she controlled to the top of the asteroid. He received his next surprise when it landed and deployed a trio of pitons attached to cables to secure it to the rock. He asked, "How in the world did you know to request that?"

She laughed. "I didn't. These happened to be what my family had lying around. They're used for mining surveys, so they often have to anchor themselves to things to gather data or samples. They have really good sensors for the same reason. We usually fire the drones into a system in a disposable missile and leave them there when their work is complete." She flipped a switch, and the main display converted to a segmented view showing the take from the units. "Even better, the software that goes with them is smart enough to combine their feeds into a combined high-resolution representation."

Jax shook his head. "I didn't know the Reardens were involved in mining."

She laughed. "You can assume we're involved in everything, in one way or another. My father has become very good at playing the shell-company shell game to avoid obvious connections. Nothing illegal, just legitimate business strategies, he'd say."

Trianna interrupted, "What the hell?"

Shapes were coming into clear resolution on the display. Jax leaned forward, having a hard time believing what he saw. "Is that what I think it is?"

Cia shook her head slowly, clearly feeling the same disbelief he was. "If you think it's a bloody space station out in the middle of nowhere, then I'd say you're right on the money."

As the huge structure's lines came into greater resolution, it became apparent that humans hadn't built it. It had a flowing, organic shape that was unlike anything he'd ever seen. "Just so I'm not crazy, that's not one of our space stations, is it? Or one of the Confederacy's?"

Trianna, who had apparently forgotten she didn't like talking to him for the moment at least, replied, "Not according to our databases. You don't think this is the big secret Alien Coalition base, do you?"

He shook his head. "Everything we know about it says that should be much deeper in their territory. What are those things around it? Ships?" As the sensors continued to pull in information, they drew the outlines of various space vessels. They were far from uniform in size, and as the detail grew it became obvious they were more dissimilar than similar in all respects.

Cia growled, "You've got to be kidding me." She hit some buttons, and a third section appeared on the main display. It contained a search program that flicked through ship profiles at a dizzying speed and compared them to the information being fed by the sensors. Whenever a match occurred, that image flew up into a box of its own along the top row. By the time it was complete, the *Occam's Cleaver* had identified seven vessels, probably a tenth of the total present. She nodded at the detail. "They're pirates. Different clans, according to our database, although that frequently changes with ship captures, mergers, and those kinds of things. Still, I can't imagine a single clan has this many ships that they can bring together like this. So what we're looking at here is a bunch of pirates hanging out in the same spot for some reason."

Jax shook his head. "Maybe this is a waypoint? Similar to the one we went to in that asteroid? Open to everyone, neutral territory?"

The pilot shrugged. "I've never heard of such a thing owned by the aliens, but it's not an unreasonable thought. Let's see if we can pick up some communication." A static hiss filled the cabin, followed by some electronic squelching sounds. It eventually transformed into radio chatter as the computer found the frequencies, but only the ordinary conversation one would expect where ships were docking and undocking with the help of station traffic control. It sounded a lot like the last place they visited. *Which means I'm probably correct.*

Athena observed, "Or it's a coincidence. It's a little too early to make assumptions based on wishful thinking."

Jax nodded. *I stand corrected.* "All right. Are we certain this is the place we're looking for?" The display shifted to show the nanoparticle detector's readings, and sure enough, the dots were clustered both in the station and on the surrounding ships. He sighed. "So, feel free to correct me if I'm wrong, but what we have here is a bunch of pirates, an alien base, and evidence that these two are somehow tied back to Arlox. Do I have it about right?"

Both pilots agreed that he did. Cia added, "Guess it's a good thing we brought all that pirate stuff aboard, huh?"

Jax nodded. "Always better to have options. Let's go tell the crew what's up."

Sirenno said, "So we get to be pirates again. Awesome. Arrrr."

Groans and laughter came from the others gathered in the galley, but Jax didn't join in. His concern about the level of danger he was exposing his people to had grown from the instant he'd realized the massive object was a space station. Reconnaissance from onboard the ship was one thing since they always had the option to run. Docking at the installation and leaving the *Cleaver* would sacrifice that relative safety. He warned, "This is going to be a lot more dangerous than I thought at the outset, folks. We need to decide if we'd be better off reporting back and waiting for reinforcements."

Marshall replied, "This is too important to delay. I say we go."

Cia countered, "Playing devil's advocate, we're talking about maybe three days before we can get support in place. Possibly less. Would that be too big a risk?"

Kimmel shrugged. "It sure seems like there are a lot of ships here. You would think if they were being brought together for a specific reason that they'd have to be nearing critical mass with this many. It's unlikely they'd arrive early and hang out for fun."

Verrand nodded. "Plus, there's no way everybody here knows everyone else. Their security will have huge holes in it because of the number of ships and people involved. I don't think it's that big a deal."

Trianna shrugged. "I always get to stay with the ship, so I'm not part of this decision. But if things go wrong and we have to blast our way out of the place, I'm totally down for that." She grinned at the idea. "I have your backs."

Jax said, "I hear all positives. So, what's the play?"

Cia replied, "The *Occam's Cleaver* is now an unaffiliated pirate ship. There's some junk in the back we can claim to have stolen, loose odds and ends that were gathering dust in one of the family warehouses. So we're visiting the station to try to sell it, or to barter the stuff for fuel and supplies."

He nodded. "We'll have to do some basic disguises in case our images are out there for whatever reason. The Academy set us up with identities for every occasion, so we're set there. Ethan and Athena can see about either inserting the records into the station's systems ahead of time or making sure when the request goes out that we intercept it."

Kimmel replied, "More likely the second one. Their internal setup is probably going to be fairly weird since it's an alien construct and all."

Athena's voice came out of the speaker in Jax's wrist comm. "We have to assume they have a network in place for the humans that visit the station, as well. It ought to give us a starting point to penetrate their systems."

Jax shrugged. "Either way, then. Let's get suited up."

Jax stood in front of the mirror in his quarters and considered the person reflected at him. He had returned to some tried-and-true tricks from his Special Forces incursion days to add a false scar that ran from above his left eye down to the cheek on that side. It noticeably pulled the surrounding skin and drew his lip up a little, causing him to speak with a slight slur. He'd added a prosthetic insert in his mouth to prevent excessive motion that might snap the scar out of place, further changing his speaking style. He'd considered shaving his head but instead settled for a quick dye job to turn his naturally dark hair blonde, shot through with grey. On the whole, he looked about ten years older and ten times meaner.

He'd dug through the clothing options they'd brought along until he'd discovered some simple patched black trousers, a heavy gun belt with holsters on either side and a dingy gray button-down shirt. A faded black vest went over it all, and when he buttoned it up, he resembled something out of an old West picture book. The pistols were Academy issue but made to look like older tech. The one at his left was energy, the one on his right, projectile. Small pouches around the belt held spare magazines and power cells. He had a blade hidden in one heel of his worn boots and a small explosive charge in the other in case they were forced to give up their weapons.

He shook his head again at the audacity of what they were about to try. Pulling off an operation like this at a human space station was one thing. Trying it in an alien facility was something else entirely. They knew nothing about what they were getting into. Still, his team was right, and in truth, he completely agreed with them. Events were moving too fast for any further delay. It was time to put the train that would eventually run over Arlox and anyone who supported him in motion.

He smiled at the man in the mirror. "Damn, you are good looking."

Athena snorted. "Narcissistic much?"

He laughed. "Tradition. I wouldn't feel right if I didn't pay my new self a compliment before we got started."

"Does that mean you're finally done primping and preening?"

He nodded and tapped his comm. "Cia, I'm ready."

"You're the last to check in. We're good to go."

"Excellent. Let's do this thing."

CHAPTER FOURTEEN

Jax spent the approach to the station in the pilot's compartment, unable to tear himself away from the possibility of receiving an early warning of trouble. Cia initiated contact. "This is the independent vessel *Occam's Cleaver*, requesting clearance and docking assignment."

There was a pause, long enough that he worried they'd missed some important protocol, before a computerized voice responded, "*Occam's Cleaver*, you're cleared for berth seventy-two A. Navigation instructions follow. Do not deviate from your assigned path or you'll be destroyed. There will be no further warning." A series of coordinates followed, and Cia tapped the screen to add them to the display as an overlay on their view of the system. It showed a looping arc that led around to the far side of the station, one that would keep them in transit for at least an hour and offer whoever was on the other side plenty of time to investigate them. *Probably deliberate. It's what I would do.*

The pilot replied, "Acknowledged. *Cleaver* out." She

looked back over her shoulder at him. "Fairly inviting bunch, really."

He nodded. "Except for the whole 'do what I say or else you die' thing."

She shrugged. "Pretty standard practice. After all, you can't trust pirates."

The slow trip in was tense but ultimately uneventful. As they rounded the far side of the station, the docking area appeared on the display. It was external to the installation's main body, a series of projections jutting out into space. Ships were attached to them like tines on a comb. Their tail ends, where cargo access was almost universally located, faced the station's projection. Some kind of shroud covered the docked vessels. The berths were mostly occupied, causing Jax to revise his estimate of the number of ships in the system. "There must be well over a hundred here."

Cia remarked, "I'm with Kimmel. This is a group getting ready to make a move."

Trianna nodded. "I agree."

Athena interjected, "Before you say it, she didn't talk to you. She still dislikes you as much as the rest of us do."

You're not a nice person. You know that? He bantered a little more with the AI on the way in, but when the shudder of connection ran through the ship as they locked onto the station, any opportunity for delay was gone. He said, with some reluctance, "Guess we better get out there."

Cia replied in a similar tone, "Guess so." She looked at Trianna. "You take care of my girl."

The copilot nodded. "As if she were my baby."

Jax didn't like the concern on Cia's face, one that he also

felt all too keenly. He managed a smile. "It'll be fine. Let's go do what you're best at: cause some trouble." Once they reached the cargo bay and joined the rest of the crew, they all watched on an external camera as a sleeve extended from the dock and stretched out to completely encapsulate the *Cleaver*. It quickly pressurized to permit them to exit the ship without suits or the need for an airlock.

Kimmel asked, "Do you think they do that even with the biggest ships? That's pretty crazy."

Cia shrugged. "I haven't seen it before, but it certainly makes sense. If it's some tough, flexible material on a roll, it seems like it wouldn't be that hard to do. Basically a giant sleeve and a zipper to connect the halves. Probably pulled into place by tiny drones or something."

Jax plowed the side of his fist into the big button that released the cargo bay door, and it slowly lowered to the deck. "Trianna, seal it up when we're gone. No one gets on for any reason without Cia's approval."

The pilot raised an eyebrow. "Couldn't have said it better myself."

Jax amended, "Or my approval. In case someone's deciding to be a problem, as usual."

Cia slapped him on the arm, and they headed out into the facility in a wash of light laughter. The initial view was boringly uniform. The metal walkway that connected the ship to the dock took a right-hand turn and became a metal floor that ran from there to the main station. A conveyor ran down the middle to transport cargo, with pedestrians required to walk along the edges. Marshall suggested, "Bet we could shorten our time by jumping on there and taking a ride."

Jax sighed. "Let's try not to cause trouble right off the bat, okay? I would have expected that from C, but not from you."

Verrand offered, "We're pirates. We do what we want."

Jax shook his head. "We're guests. How about we avoid ticking off our hosts?"

She scowled. "You're no fun at all."

He shrugged. "So I've been told." They passed other humans walking in the opposite direction, presumably returning to their ships' berths. The scale of the installation was immense, far more extensive than it had seemed from the outside. He shook his head. "I can't believe this place is hanging out here in the middle of nowhere. It's really impressive."

Athena warned, "As expected, audio and video surveillance is present in the corridor, and presumably throughout the facility. I found the human network and negotiated outer layer access, but Kimmel is correct about the main system architecture being foreign to my experience. It would be far too risky to attempt to intrude upon it."

More or less what we expected. How much can you get out of the human network?

"Basic information, station layout, that sort of thing. Nothing that will lead us directly to any of our objectives."

Damn. Okay. Let's do what normal pirates would do, then, and head toward wherever the main center of commerce is on this thing. After all, we have loot to sell, supplies to buy, and hopefully food to eat.

The map Athena accessed listed several areas on the station that could qualify as primary commercial zones. He chose the one nearest to their entry point, figuring it was logical to have humans dock closest to human amenities and have aliens do the same. While he was deeply curious about what species had constructed the installation, he felt no pressing need to run into any of them. Hopefully, they'd get a sense of the beings behind it before they departed, but he wasn't going to put his people in a situation where they might unwittingly cross a behavioral line they didn't have the understanding to see in the first place.

The commercial area occupied a portion of the station's main structure, which Athena's schematics suggested was a stack of circular levels rising from the bottom of the station to the top. The one on this level featured a two-story ceiling with ample lighting above and a series of lanes large enough for four people walking side by side that ran between small stands. It looked more like a temporary bazaar than a space housing permanent shops. The presence of various pirate clan symbols and rickety-looking tables with wares spread out across them supported that interpretation.

The pathways ran on a diagonal toward the middle, with concentric rings at intervals that created strangely shaped blocks. He led the team idly through them and announced, "Food first. Shopping later. Maybe we'll find some eats near the core." It made sense that if any enduring shop existed in the area, it would be a restaurant, or dare he hope, a bar. When they reached the end of the lane, it revealed a much larger section than he'd anticipated. Seats were scattered in the center in clusters, two here, eight there, and singles all around, arranged seemingly at random. The tables themselves weren't uniform either. Some were round, some square, some rectangular, and one was a strange trapezoid. He said to Cia, "Maybe you should see if you could get that one for the *Cleaver*. Might make a nice card table."

She shook her head. "I'm comfortable with what we've got, thanks. Besides, you know we don't like to talk about your *gambling problem*." She whispered the last words as loudly as she could, then her voice returned to normal. "What's that smell?"

He sniffed the air and caught the scent she referred to, a mix of spices and cooking meat. He surveyed the area and spotted food stands arrayed around the edges of the circle that offered cuisines from more planets than he'd visited during his career, to judge by the signs. His nose led him to a kebab stand, where chunks of meat separated by vegetables were being cooked over an open flame. "What's in that?"

The heavyset woman in dingy chef's whites grinned at him. "Only the best. It's a camel analogue from the Xantian system, and the vegetables are green peppers, tomatoes, and zucchini." He glanced back at his crew, who all looked as hungry as he was. He turned to the cook. "We'll take ten for starters."

She nodded. "Ship name?"

"*Occam's Cleaver*."

She barked a laugh. "Interesting name. Fancy, but meaningless to anyone other than you all, I suppose."

He shrugged. "Wasn't my choice. Came with the pilot."

She grinned. "That's what they all say after they make a

bad decision. I'll charge the meal back to your vessel." She handed over a tray filled with disposable plates holding kebabs. "Some rice to go with it?"

"With something that smells as amazing as this, I don't want to waste my appetite on anything else."

She shook her head but seemed happy. "Off with you. You know where to find me when you're ready for seconds."

They gathered at a table that had the appropriate number of chairs and dug in. As they ate, Jax said, "So, how's this? C and K check out where we can sell our cargo, start getting an idea of prices. V and I will look around the station areas near here and see what luxuries are available. I'm leaning toward spending our sleeping hours on the ship, but maybe there's a hotel or something that would give us a reason not to." *Like an access point we could use, for instance.*

Athena replied, "Unlikely. I haven't detected any. It appears Ethan's insistence that everyone carry an adapter is for naught."

Well, it doesn't hurt to look. And while we're looking, you can also try to narrow in on people who are carrying nanoparticles. We need to find someone in a position of authority who might know what's going on, then have a serious conversation with them.

She replied, "That would require sending out an active instruction to initiate a response from them. Do you want to risk it?"

Yes, once. I don't want to wait for tomorrow morning's data. Out loud, he finished, "The rest of you go shopping. You know what's essential to survival, what's necessary for reasonable comfort, and what's on our expanded wish list. See if you can find some of it. I'm guessing this place is our best option. If it doesn't work out, we'll try going up or down a level."

The meal ended when they'd consumed every single bit of food. Then they split up. Jax and Verrand headed for the large hallway that led to the adjoining areas outside the central column. As they walked, Athena updated him on her progress in navigating the installation's computer system. "I've managed to access a real-time schematic, rather than the static one I had before. There's little difference, but I can use it to overlay the data from the ping." She did so, and he checked the display on his comm. It showed nanoparticles all over the place.

Wow. Seriously? Do you think it's possible there's a government agent here who spread it to all these people?

The AI replied, "No way to tell at all. I wouldn't even hazard a guess."

He nodded. *Okay, there's a cluster there that's denser than the rest. Let's give that a try.*

They followed Athena's directions, transmitted through their earpieces, and eventually found two very interesting things. The first was a dark, crowded, and loud bar. Jax grinned. "My kind of place."

Verrand wore a satisfied smile. "Mine too. Looks like we get drinks up there." She pointed to a long bar that ran along one side of the room and led the way toward it. Tall and short tables filled the rest of the space, the former for standing, the latter for sitting.

The other item of interest was the location of the nanoparticle cluster. Despite the fact that such a thing would've been highly unlikely in this particular bar, his brain had locked on the idea that he'd find some government bigwig surrounded by more government people. Maybe intelligence, maybe military, perhaps something else. But something official.

The sight that greeted him definitely *wasn't* official. Sharing space with the dots was a band of hardened-looking pirates who laughed and drank like they didn't have a care in the world. The one at the head of their table was clearly their leader, as evidenced by tiny gold rings indicating his rank that embraced the long mustaches drooping to either side of his chin.

For a moment, Jax had no idea what to say, and Verrand took the lead. "Okay, that's unexpected. Guess we need to go have a conversation with some of our fellow pirates." She handed him his drink and headed off in their direction.

CHAPTER FIFTEEN

The man caught sight of them when they were halfway across the room. His body didn't betray his attention, but Jax saw his eyes flick to Verrand, dart away, then return to her. A faint smile creased the edges of the pirate's lips. She strode forward and stopped right next to him, taking the initiative. "Hiya. Couldn't help but notice that you've got an impressive looking crew here."

The man nodded. He had long dark hair to complement the mustaches, and wrinkles from age and experience lined his face. His skin was a medium tan, and it nicely offset the bright white button-down shirt he wore. "Aye, we're a pretty solid bunch, I'd say." He glanced down the length of the table and asked, "Wouldn't you agree?"

The crowd with him, presumably members of his crew, banged their mugs on the table and cheered. Their leader looked up at Verrand with a smile. "So, now that we've got that out of the way, what can I do for you?"

She shrugged. "A little conversation maybe?"

He waved a hand at an unoccupied chair at a nearby

table. "Pull up a seat. Afraid there's no room for your friend, though." He smirked at Jax as he said it.

Jax nodded at the other man. "No worries. I'm happy to stand. Makes me feel powerful."

The pirate laughed. "If you need such trappings to feel powerful, then you aren't actually powerful."

Jax grinned. "Ah, but it's not always easy to see power. Sometimes one must display it ostentatiously." He stared at the rings in the man's facial hair as he said it.

"True enough. You can call me Rachi." Verrand sat and gave the man their false names. She continued, "So, this is my ship's first time here. What can you tell us about this spot?"

He shrugged. "Pretty standard station, although non-humans run it."

Jax asked, "Is it a Coalition place? One of our crew thought maybe it was *the* Coalition place, but it seems too far out near the border to be that."

The man nodded and stroked his mustaches. "I've heard that question a time or two as well. While I've never been deep enough into Coalition territory to verify it, I can't imagine this is their main headquarters. I've seen several alien races here though, too many to decisively say whether it's one of them behind the place's creation and operation, or more than one." He shrugged. "It kind of doesn't matter. Cash spends, supplies are available, and hardly anyone finds the need to escalate fights beyond fists." He looked pointedly at the guns on Jackson's hips.

"That's good to hear. I was surprised when the weapons were allowed."

One of the man's crew members, a woman with short

blonde hair, laughed. "That's because you haven't seen the inside of their cells. Let me tell you, firing a weapon in this place is a bad, bad idea."

Verrand looked doubtful. "Really?"

The pirate captain, for that was surely what he was based on the deference the others showed, nodded. "Minimum six months, and not a comfortable six months either. That's for a first offense that harms no one."

Jax whistled. "That *is* steep. Think I'll keep these babies right where they are." He patted his pistols.

"Good choice." The other man returned his attention to Verrand. "So, what's your ship?"

"The *Occam's Cleaver*. We're independent at the moment, but not sure we want to stay that way."

"You the captain?"

She shook her head. "No, but he's not so great with words. Tends to think with his muscles, so I try to do most of the talking. I'm the ship's second."

The man looked up at Jax. "I presume she's referring to you?"

He nodded. "What I lack in brilliance, I make up for in sheer personality."

The pirate laughed and raised his glass in a toast. "I'll drink to that." He did, and his crew matched him.

Verrand said, "I know this is a little bold, but if we were considering joining up with an organization, would you have a recommendation?"

He shrugged. "Our clan's pretty solid and has been for some time. We don't take on newcomers without a probation period, of course. Standard rules, percentage goes up the chain. When you find good people to join, you receive a part of their tithes as a finder's fee."

She nodded. "Makes sense. Maybe we could get together to talk about it at a later time? When we're not in quite such a busy place?"

He laughed again. "You'll learn soon there's no privacy on this station. Someone's always watching or listening. But sure, we can talk sometime."

She pressed, "Aboard your ship perhaps?"

He shook his head. "Darlin', we don't know each other that well yet." He put heavy innuendo in the tone, and his crew burst into laughter.

Verrand smiled. "Fair enough. Maybe we can find neutral ground at one of the hotels around here or whatever. Okay if I look for you tomorrow?"

"Sure. But don't start looking until late. We'll be celebrating here for a while." His subordinates whooped and cheered again.

She nodded. "Sounds good." She rose and headed toward a different corner of the room. Jax followed while waving goodbye to the pirate, who lifted his chin in acknowledgment.

When he caught up with her, he leaned close so they wouldn't be overheard and activated his comm so the rest of the crew could listen in. "Not bad for first contact with a potential partner." He stressed the last word so everyone would understand that he was speaking of a target. "I'm not sure he'll be into talking to us further though, despite your smooth chatter."

Verrand shook her head. "They're sure to be pretty secretive about their business. Probably we need another three or four casual encounters before we would get down to something serious."

Cia quipped, "Is he handsome? You could take one for the team, then."

She laughed. "Attractive enough, maybe, if he spent some significant time in the shower. But let's consider that a very last resort, shall we?"

Chuckles came back over the comm. Athena added, "Station records don't have any data on him or his crew. I've discovered many of the ships are in a similar situation and presume they have likely paid to remain anonymous."

Kimmel asked, "Rather than doing it themselves?"

She replied, "If I can't pull that off, I doubt they can."

Jax snorted. *Now who's a narcissist?*

The AI countered, speaking only in his head, "It's not narcissism to acknowledge I should be able to defeat whatever systems are available here. Since I cannot manage that task, it stands to reason that such a thing is impossible and thus must've been accomplished by another means. It's logic, Jax. You might want to look it up sometime."

Uh-huh. Sure. He changed the subject and addressed the team. "So, I think we're going to have to do a little extra work to get close to these people since they so rudely rejected our overture. Let's finish up what we're doing, maybe grab another couple kebabs, and head back to the *Cleaver* for the night. We'll figure out our plans from there."

After a good night's sleep, the crew gathered in the galley. Jax began, "So, we have a bunch of pirates who are connected to Arlox somehow, based on their exposure to the nanoparticles. We need to find out more about them."

Kimmel suggested, "If we figure out what ship he's on, we can try to hack into it."

Jax replied, "Okay, that's one thing for the to-do list. What else have you people got?"

Cia shrugged. "Once we know which ship is his, we could try to bug it if hacking doesn't succeed. I have some devices that would work."

Marshall countered, "Even through jump?"

The pilot lifted a hand and rocked it back and forth. "Maybe. Okay, probably not. They put out a unique signal, but without having an idea where to look, stumbling upon it would be pretty difficult."

Sirenno interjected, "Could Athena modify whatever we used with the nanoparticles to work with the device? Send something over the networks instead of blasting a signal out through space?"

Athena replied over the comm, "Unfortunately, no. Not without access to more resources than we have here."

Verrand offered, "We could probably find what you need."

"It's not a question of the actual physical materials, but of the precision fabrication required to create the modifications. As far as I know, that's only available at the Academy."

Cia asked, "Maybe a tool shop here on the station?"

Jax shook his head. "There's no explainable reason we would need to find one, and we have to assume they'd be watching. I sure would be in their place. So, that's out."

Athena reported, "The morning's ping came through.

I've identified the location of their ship. Fortunately, most of them are on board, right here." The display on the wall shifted to show a schematic of the space station. The pirates were docked several levels above the *Cleaver* and a little closer to the structure's central portion.

Jax replied, "Good. That's a step in the correct direction. Okay, how about we do this? We have some old-school surveillance devices packed away. Tiny audio transmitters and receivers, that sort of thing. Let's dig through them, make sure everybody has some, then try to plant them on members of his crew. Maria and I will need to opt out of that project, so we don't get recognized and blow the game."

Athena warned, "The likelihood that such transmissions would be detected is impossible to calculate since we know nothing about the alien technology at the heart of this solution."

"Dammit," Jax growled.

Kimmel sounded thoughtful. "What if we were able to dial back the transmissions? Make it so they only travel a very short distance? It would require us to get a listener in position nearby, but then that person could share the feed over the comm so we could all hear it. Is it safe to assume our comms are secure?"

Athena replied, "Almost certainly. They are heavily encoded and use an unusual frequency."

Jax inquired, "Athena, Ethan, can you alter the devices?"

The AI confirmed, "Yes, almost certainly."

He nodded decisively. "Okay, that's the plan then. Let's get at least one listening device for everyone, then get out there and wait for them to move. When they do, we get as many bugs as we can on them, then each of us follows one of them around. After you all bug him, I'll track the captain."

Cia protested, "Didn't you just say that was dangerous?"

Jax gave a wide grin. "This is what I do. As long as I don't need to get within arm's length, he'll never see me."

CHAPTER SIXTEEN

Jax wandered the shops and stands of the bazaar, idly examining the items being peddled while his attention focused on the reports coming in through his earpiece. The team had planted listening devices on several crew members, and Cia was nearing the captain. He regretted for the first time during the trip that Juno hadn't come along because her deft hands would've had the best chance at planting a bug on the pirate leader without detection. The plan was for the pilot to bump into him and attach it to his clothing—an oldie, but a goodie. Marshall was nearby, ready to intervene if something went wrong. Still, Jax wished it could be him there, either delivering the bug or backing up his friend. *Can't have everything, I guess.*

Athena replied, "This is true. I'm sure it will all work out fine."

He laughed inwardly. *That's very optimistic. Kind of rare for you.*

"I have a good feeling about it."

Her faith was rewarded a moment later as Cia reported, "It's on him. No issues."

Jax nodded and walked toward Cia's location, following Athena's directions. He picked up the pirate captain as the man entered a long hallway and dawdled at the entrance to allow his target to gain a solid lead. Rachi was headed toward one of the hotels, which seemed strange given that he and most of his crew had bunked aboard ship, and spoke of potentially interesting goings-on.

He ensured a substantial batch of people remained between him and his target. Despite what he'd said to the others about his stalking prowess, the scar would make him more noticeable. The bandana that covered his blonde hair and a casual shirt and denim pants rendered him very different-looking than he'd been at their previous meeting, and he was confident he could remain undetected. His pistols and the belt that held them were back on the ship, and while he felt naked without the weapons, they were too identifiable to wear on an operation requiring any measure of subtlety.

The man went into a hotel called Smugglers Respite. Jax walked past the entrance and stopped three businesses down while pretending to look at the bar's menu. *Athena, any surveillance access inside?*

"No. Everything is wired into the main system, which I cannot get into. Believe me; it's as frustrating to me as it is to you."

Marshall sauntered down the hallway toward him. Jax covered his mouth with his hand and muttered, "Let's leapfrog. You go in, find out where he's going, then I'll follow them."

The other man nodded an affirmative and turned into the hotel. After several minutes, he said, "Dude's walking in the direction of a large conference room on the first level, and a lot of the people here seem like they're headed there too. A lot of people who look like pirates."

Cia suggested, "Could be a clan meeting. If so, they'd want neutral ground, which could explain why they didn't choose a ship. Maybe doing it there guarantees them some level of privacy. You never know, if they bribed the station to keep them out of the systems, they could easily have paid off the hotel to kill some cameras."

Jax asked, "Any obvious spot where I can get close?"

Marshall replied, "Can't be sure. But there are a lot of doors down that hall. I'm heading out now."

Jax avoided eye contact as they passed one another in the hotel doorway. He strode forward down the only corridor leading from the lobby, keeping his head up and trying to look like he belonged. The room Marshall had referred to was immediately obvious. Groups of pirates stood outside it in clusters, talking among themselves and shooting suspicious glances at anyone who wasn't part of their little bunch.

He muttered apologies as he threaded through the groups and spared the conference room a glance in passing before turning his face away. It held a large conference table surrounded by chairs, each of them filled. Standing behind each seat was a group of individuals who looked younger or less authoritative than those in front of them, and he concluded it was probably a meeting of ship captains with crew members in support. *Which might mean that some other people who would recognize me are here.*

The next door down was unlocked, and he pulled it open and ducked inside. Chairs were stacked along one side of the walk-in closet, and a tall set of shelves holding banquet equipment covered the other with everything from cups to plates to massive coffee urns. He flipped the switch on the handle to lock the door, then sat on the floor with his back against the meeting room's wall. He activated the audio receiver and heard voices, but a wavering interference rendered them unintelligible. *Athena, what's going on?*

"They have a scrambler or white noise device in there to mess with transmissions. Standby." After several seconds, she instructed, "Adjust the setting to three-nine-seven mark four." He complied, and the feed cleaned up immediately.

What did you do?

"I'm using your comm to transmit an inverted version of their scrambler signal. At this frequency, the two combine and cancel one another out."

Jax routed the ungarbled audio feed into his comm so the rest of the team could listen in. The sound of pounding came from the room beyond, and the pirate they'd planted the bug on spoke. "All right, people. I come before you with a proposition. We've all been brought together for a reason, and we've given our word that we'll participate in the upcoming attack. What the fools who recruited us have forgotten is that we're pirates."

Laughter rang out, accompanied by cheering and hooting loud enough to be heard through the wall. When it died down, the man continued, "I'm not saying that those of you who wish to continue shouldn't do so. As always, we in Clan Shimsa can choose our path as long as the money continues to flow. But in this case, I suggest we decide to act together because by doing so we can reap a reward far greater than what we've been promised."

Another voice, older-sounding and hoarse, interjected, "Rachi, get on with it, will you? We've got drinking to do." More laughter came across the audio feed.

The pirate leader chuckled. "Certainly. Here's my idea. When we gather at the rally point before the attack to take on supplies, we turn this thing on its head." The side conversations that had been a dull rumble under his voice fell away. "If our intelligence is correct, a large number of undermanned ships will be there with us. So here's what we'll do. Before the go signal comes, we send out boarding teams, breach those ships, and take them for ourselves. Then we get the hell out of there before they know what's going on."

A voice filled with doubt and a touch of condescension asked, "Won't that get us blacklisted?"

The pirate leader laughed. "Like we would care about such a thing. If I never work for a government again, it's of no matter to me. I can't see them increasing their efforts to interfere with us. They have too many things to attend to, and that doesn't look to change. Especially after the fallout from what they've got planned."

Cia whispered, "What do you think he means about undercrewed ships?"

Jax shook his head. "No idea, but I don't like the sound of it." In the past, he'd encountered vessels with skeleton crews that were used as battering rams primed to explode when they made contact. It was costly but effective.

The pirate captain asked, "So, what do you say?" The discussion lasted for about ten minutes as they debated the pros and cons before silence fell again. He requested formally, "Captains, please register your responses."

One after another, different voices spoke the word "Aye." None of them argued against the proposal. When the vote was complete, the leader said, "Excellent. I'm sorry to say that the drinking will have to be put on hold, Escante, because we need to get ourselves into position ahead of the rest to stake out the best locations near the most compelling targets."

Jax bolted to his feet and left the storeroom to ensure he was past the conference room before any pirates exited it. He muttered, low and urgent, "I thought we would have more time. Athena, is there any way we can bug their ship so we know where it's going?"

Over the comm, the AI responded, "No. We don't have any such technology available."

Jax cursed inwardly. "What about following them?"

Trianna replied, "We could get out ahead of them if everyone hoofed it back to the ship. But if they jump, we won't have any idea where they go."

Jax shook his head. "Then there's only one option. I have to take him down before he can get to his ship, and we need to sneak him onto the *Cleaver*. Then we can interrogate him on the way to wherever they're supposed to go."

There were gasps of surprise, and Marshall stated, "I'll come and assist."

Jax, who had found a place to stand where he could watch anyone coming out of the hotel without being noticed, shook his head slightly. "Negative. I have something else for you to do." Rachi emerged with the blonde woman and a burly man who'd been at the table with him in the bar. All three had batons strapped to their belts in addition to the pistols they carried. *Dammit, I should've brought a weapon.*

Athena reminded him, "You have two, attached to your shoulders."

True enough. Okay, I want you to figure out where my best opportunity to get them is, based on where we're going. He dipped into his pocket and pulled out his display glasses, no longer concerned that they would give him away since secrecy was likely about to be a thing of the past, anyway. "The rest of you get back to the ship, except for Verrand and Marshall. You two find something to move him in once I've got him, a rolling crate, a barrel, a bloody coffin, I don't care. Anything we can use to get him to the ship alive will work."

Affirmatives sounded, and he followed his target. No opportunity to act presented itself before they entered the long hallway that led to the ships, and Jax cursed under his breath. The crowd thinned out the further they traveled, diminishing his ability to follow without being seen. Athena said, "You only have about thirty seconds before we'll be visible to the ship."

He tensed himself to rush forward, but as he was about to take the first step, a trio of humans rounded the corner and called out to his target. Jax knelt to fasten the straps on his boot and surreptitiously watched as they joined the party. *Dammit, there's no way I can do it now. I can't believe we've come this far only to lose them.* He ordered, "Verrand, Marshall, get to the *Cleaver*. You all do your best to stay close to the ship without spooking it on the trip out."

Cia's voice came over the comm, with her copilot negotiating departure details with the station barely audible in the background. "Jax. Tell me you're not about to do something stupid."

"Me? Never." He shuffled ahead to the edge of the tube that led to the pirate ship and peered around the corner. They had mounted the cargo ramp, and the area beyond it was filled with crates from floor to ceiling aside from a narrow lane heading forward. His eyes widened at the sight of boxes marked with the UCCA logo. "Holy hell. These bastards are part of the same group we saw on the other station, Cia. They have Alliance material on board that looks exactly like the other stuff."

He had intended to get a last look and run for the *Occam's Cleaver* on the off chance he might make it before they obeyed his instructions to depart. That was no longer an option. Too much was coming together, and they couldn't risk allowing the knowledge the crew of that ship held to escape them. The captain slapped the button to close the cargo door on the pirate's vessel and walked away, and his people followed. The ramp started to rise.

Athena, give me all the jolt I can handle. He dashed forward in a low run to avoid anyone on board seeing the motion. Energy surged through him and gave him an extra boost of speed. When he was close enough, he leapt at the closing ramp, caught the edge with his fingertips, and used the strength in his enhanced arms to launch himself up and over. He fell down the far side of it and slammed hard onto the deck in the small area between the rear door and the stacked crates. No sooner was the ramp secure than a shudder ran through the vessel as it detached from the station.

Jax breathed, "Stay close, people. Signing off for a while." He deactivated his comm lest the outgoing signal be detected and wiggled around until he was in a halfway comfortable position. *Athena, I know I got us into this, but we'll need to work together to find a way to get us out of it.*

She laughed. "Big surprise. That's always the way it works with you, Jax."

CHAPTER SEVENTEEN

Jax remained quietly in place in his little nook at the back of the cargo bay for a full fifteen minutes. He scrunched into as small a shape as possible and made sure to cover his skin so if a camera were present in the area, it would see an amorphous lump rather than a body. *Athena, anything?*

"No. I can't detect the ship's network. If I had to guess, they have the wireless functions turned off. I've never heard of such a thing."

Jax nodded. *I have. Our ships have done it before when going into particularly hot combat situations. If you know that everyone's wired in, you can eliminate the possibility of anyone hacking in by wireless. They probably had it off as extra security at the station and will turn it back on once they're in jump. I don't think we can afford to wait, though.*

"I have no reason to argue with your assessment."

Then I guess it's time to look around. He moved slowly and carefully as he climbed into a crouch and crept forward to the aisle that ran back through the cargo containers toward the main part of the ship. The only sounds that reached his ears were the familiar creaks and thrums of a vessel under power, which was reassuring. The craft had gravity, but it would still make sense for most of the crew to be strapped in at their stations or in their quarters in case of sudden maneuvering, especially if they didn't trust the other ships in the system. *No honor among pirates, right? This bunch definitely lives by that mantra.* He moved slowly and silently up the aisle and discovered a closed bulkhead door on the far side. The configuration was different from the *Grace*, where the cargo area opened directly onto the living areas. *I take it this ship is bigger than ours?*

"About fifteen percent larger, yes."

Where would I be most likely to find a place to jack in? He said a small word of thanks in his mind to Kimmel for insisting they all continue to carry the adapters.

"We can probably assume there will be some in operational areas. The fact that they're currently operating without wireless would suggest system connection points all over the ship."

Like on the oldest military vessels. You'd wear your headset and plug it in wherever you happen to be working. Makes sense. He put his ear to the door and listened but heard nothing beyond it. *Here goes.* Like many vacuum-rated doors, this one had physical handles instead of an electronic mechanism that might fail catastrophically if the system went out. He moved the levers as quietly as possible and winced at the slight screech that each gave. *Maintenance procedures could be better.*

"You're one to talk. When was the last time you did anything to help freshen up the *Grace*?"

Shut it. The door opened outward, and he pushed it far

enough to look into the area beyond. When he didn't see any immediate threat, he opened it the rest of the way and discovered paths leading to the right, left, and forward, presumably down the ship's centerline. *Probably makes more sense to go to a side, don't you think?*

"Less chance of running into someone moving from one part of the ship to another, I agree."

He closed the door carefully behind him and rotated the latches back into place, then headed to the left. The corridor ended at a bulkhead with a door to the right. This one wasn't vacuum-rated, and he paused before activating the sensor to listen again. Hearing nothing, he readied himself for what might lie beyond it and passed his hand over the illuminated panel. The door slid aside and revealed a small storage area filled with straps, bolts, and heavy tools secured to the walls. Better, a workbench ran along the side that faced the center of the ship, and above it, a port to connect to the network. *Yes.* He turned to lock the door, but right before he hit the switch, he thought better of it. *Athena, how likely is it that a locked door will show up on a sensor board somewhere?*

"It's guaranteed. The question is whether the crew will be monitoring the board or whether there's a notification system set up to alert them. I wouldn't risk it."

Agreed. He withdrew the adapter from his pocket and slotted it into the wall, then returned to stand next to the door, ready to deal with anyone who might come through. His display glasses showed lines of code swirling as Athena navigated her way into the system. Several moments later, a schematic of the ship appeared. "I'm in."

What level of access?

"I have outer layer permissions, which means I can read almost anything unless it's on a specifically secured server, but I have limited ability to take action. I'm worming my way into those privileges, but it will take some time."

Understood. Can you show me the external view?

A window opened in his visual field to show a sensor representation of the area around them. Several ships were in motion to the jump point, and the *Occam's Cleaver* had indeed gotten out ahead of the pirate ship. She was moving slowly enough that the pirate ship would likely catch up to them before the jump. *That's a bold play if they have any suspicions at all.*

Athena agreed. "Certainly, but it's logical to assume the pirates would look for pursuers behind, rather than in front. Logical, but still a dangerous choice."

Jax reviewed the schematic, which had small labels indicating the purpose of each room on the map. He took special note of the armory and several supply areas that might contain EVA gear should he need it. He wasn't about to try the arsenal until Athena gained full access to the ship systems. If the crew was watching any compartment on board, that would be the one. *Can you get into the navigation system to see where we're heading?*

"Negative. All bridge systems require a markedly higher level of permission. I have to move slowly on them so they don't notice my intrusion."

I understand. Different question. Let's say we're on this thing through jump. How can we be sure that the Grace *can follow us?*

She was silent for a time. "I've reviewed the ship's systems and find nothing we can use to accomplish that goal. However, we do have one unique resource in place. The nanoparticles."

Jax frowned. If she expected him to perform the mental leap to understand her intention, her expectations were too high. *More likely she's trying to make me feel stupid*, he thought, careful not to let that one reach the level of consciousness that Athena shared. *How does that help us?*

"If we trigger a ping from the nanoparticles at different intervals, the other members of the team would be able to detect the signal if they were looking for it. We could theoretically bracket the normal ping so we're sure that they are."

He thought about it. It made sense: it was unlikely to be detected as long as they didn't overuse it, and the others would indeed be on the lookout for it. *Okay, that sounds like a good idea. Now the problem is making sure the others know we have a plan, so they don't try anything crazy at the jump point to rescue us.*

Amusement entered the AI's tone. "You really think they like you enough to rescue you? They're probably throwing a party right now."

Hush. Can you access the comm system, or the external lights, or something that would allow us to get a message to them?

"I could, but again, we have no guarantee it would remain hidden. If the pirates have security subroutines running, it's entirely possible they would be on the lookout for such things. As an arguably suspicious bunch, you would think that pirate captains would be more likely to keep an eye on their crew than a normal ship would."

Yes, very true. Okay, let's do one ping followed by two pings a minute later. Hopefully, the system will alert them to the first one, and they'll be watching for the second. Sure, there will be a delay while it bounces around the networks, but it shouldn't take that long. Do you see any flaws?

"In you? Too many to list. In that plan, only a few, but I agree it's our best shot. The only question I would ask is whether you believe they are truly likely to act before the ship jumps, since we could do the same thing once we arrive at our destination."

I think they will. For all they know, they're about to lose sight of me entirely. While I'm not all that important in the grand scheme of things, you definitely are. I wouldn't put it past Maarsen to have said a quiet word to one or more of them about making sure you don't fall into anyone else's hands, regardless of what it might cost me.

He didn't often hear surprise in her tone, but he did now. "You believe the Professor would prioritize my existence over yours?"

Absolutely. That doesn't mean I think he'd throw away my life cavalierly. Still, if it comes down to a choice between saving a half-human, half-mechanical Special Forces captain and preserving the most advanced artificial intelligence ever to have existed, he'll come down on the side of saving you. I would do the same thing. While Cia might have a problem with it, I think the rest of the crew would understand. Now that we've discussed it, I wouldn't be at all surprised if Trianna is the one he leaned on for it.

"Because she doesn't like you?"

She likes me fine. She has a problem showing it. No, because she's the least connected to the rest of us. It would feel the least like betrayal if she was the one. Plus, she knows how to pilot the ship. It would be easy enough for her to lock Cia out at a pivotal moment, assuming the Academy planted some sort of backdoor into the Grace's systems.

"I find that unlikely."

Unlikely, but far from impossible, so let's assume that's going to be the situation. Do the pings.

After the first signal, he requested that Athena zoom in his display to show the Grace. Her disguise as the Occam's Cleaver really is convincing. Even knowing it was the same ship, he couldn't make out any of the original lines on the counterfeit vessel. Thirty seconds after the double ping went out, the ship's engines fluttered for an instant, and her wings rocked back and forth almost imperceptibly.

Jax grinned. Message received. All right. Now, let's go back into the cargo bay and see if we can find a crate with some food in it. I'm starving, and heaven only knows how long we'll be in transition after we jump. The one thing he knew was that once they arrived wherever they were going, his friends would be sure to follow.

CHAPTER EIGHTEEN

Within an hour of entering jump, the pirates had restored wireless, and Athena had secured access to all the ship's systems except the most well-protected ones. Being able to see the crew's movements allowed Jax to move more freely around the vessel, and he discovered a better hiding place near an airlock. Once he'd figured out the lay of the land, he made short trips out to secure supplies, including food, drinks, and an EVA suit. It wasn't the quality he was used to, certainly not in the Special Forces, and not even in the Academy, but it would do in a pinch. *And this is definitely a pinch.*

He ran his hands over it methodically and automatically. The check to make sure all the seals were tight was a long-standing habit from years in the military. Maintaining equipment was one of the ways soldiers whiled away the work hours between battles. Athena gave him a look into the ship's life on his display glasses, and he watched the pirates eat, drink and carouse, and keep a surprisingly rigorous and businesslike bridge watch. While the crew didn't approach the precision of the people he generally worked with, for a group whose lives were probably mostly spent aboard ship, they seemed to have discovered an effective balance between business and pleasure.

The atmosphere shifted more toward the former after about six hours in jump space, which Jax took as a sign that they neared their exit. He climbed into the vacuum suit and asked Athena to give him an external view.

When the ship reverted, he saw that the pirate captain's expectations had been pretty much on the mark. According to the navigational data Athena had procured, their destination was another system in the middle of nowhere. In the center of the emptiness lay a huge tender, a military ship whose sole purpose was to service other ships. Arranged around it in unsteady lines were a bunch of smaller vessels. As he watched, one exited the facility to be quickly replaced by another sliding into the opposite end of the large hangar on the near side of the rectangular box that was the tender's main structure. There would be an identical hangar on the far side if it were the ship class he thought it was. *They're going in for supplies on one end and coming out the other ready to go.*

Athena confirmed his observation and added, "This ship has received its assignment. We should be inside the station in about seven hours."

Wow. That seems like a long time.

"It may be because the ships in the sector are an unusually diverse variety of sizes and types than a tender like this would normally service. It probably takes longer to shift the proper materials into place and get them loaded."

Any evidence that the surrounding ships are short on crew?

Athena replied, "I have no way to tell. I don't have access to life science sensors on the ship, and since they're hanging there, determining whether they're mechanically or physically piloted is also impossible."

And it could easily enough be a full crew allowing the computers to do the piloting, anyway. He shrugged. *Guess we'll have to wait for the* Grace *to get that information for us. Speaking of which, three pings, then three more after a minute.*

"Will do."

Do you know what the other two pods that Cia had installed are?

The AI laughed. "Yes."

Are you going to tell me?

"No. She wouldn't like that."

He shook his head. Whose side are you on, anyway?

"Why, Cia's, of course. Was that not obvious?"

You wound me. Deeply. The pain is almost unbearable. Alert me if something interesting happens. He closed his eyes and drifted into a light sleep.

When Athena prodded him back into consciousness, he checked the comm and discovered several hours had passed. *Why did you wake me up?*

"*Occam's Cleaver* has entered the system."

He sat up, rubbed his eyes, and slipped his glasses on again. *All right, about time. Can you connect me?*

"Yes, standby."

A few seconds later, his earpiece signaled a connection. "Cia?"

The pilot's voice was among the most welcome things he'd ever heard. "Of course. You didn't think we'd let you steal all the glory for yourself, did you?"

He laughed. "Where are you?"

"On the outskirts. It'll take us a couple of hours to get near you, but I wanted to make sure they didn't notice us entering the area."

"Good choice. This place is some sort of arming and refueling station. It'll be our pirate friends' turn soon, and once we're inside, I'm going to get the hell off this boat."

"Then what?"

"We'll figure out the timing; then you'll plan to get here about thirty minutes or so after we enter. That'll give me enough time to find out what's going on and locate a way out to you. That tender is bound to have escape pods or something I can use. I fly out, you catch me, and we're out of here."

He heard the frown in her voice. "How do you think we're going to catch you?"

He shrugged. "I figure that's your problem. I'm sure you can match speed and direction and catch me with a rope or a net or something. Ask Marshall. He'll come up with a way to do it that makes him the hero of the day."

Cia snorted. "You're not wrong there."

"I'm going to kill this channel and stay silent until I have information to share. I'll turn it on at half-hour intervals for one minute, so if you need to reach me you'll be able to."

"Affirmative. *Cleaver* out." The connection switched off, and he settled back against the bulkhead with a sigh. *Okay, Athena, what's our timetable?*

She replied, "We should be in the facility in seventy minutes, give or take."

Okay, send that in a burst when the next conversation

window opens. That form of communication would be even harder to detect since it was a squeal of data rather than an ongoing signal. He considered what lay ahead. *What do you think about getting into the armory?*

"I think it's a bad idea. You're not likely to win a shootout when you get off the ship. If you did, there's no way you can take on their whole vessel. You'll have to pretend to be a mouse. A *little* mouse. With cute ears."

He grumbled inwardly, but she was right. *You don't think there might be some stun stuff in there that would make it worth the effort?*

"It's far less likely that you would find stun gear on a pirate ship than you would on the tender. If you were determined to take the risk in one place or the other, I'd say better to delay it. Besides, our objective isn't on this ship. It's on the other one. You're bored and want to do something."

Yeah, I know. By the time the pirate ship finally entered the tender, his boredom had reached its pinnacle. He forced himself to wait and watch as the pirates redistributed themselves throughout the vessel to assist with the refueling and rearming. Finally, he slipped out the bottom airlock, fully cognizant it would probably set off an alarm somewhere in the ship but no longer able to delay taking action.

He strode away from the vessel with purpose, his hands itching for the weapons that were missing from his belt. The helmet was transparent but sufficiently dingy and scarred that he wasn't overly worried about being recognized. He'd peeled off the fake scar and ditched the mouth prosthetic, so if one of the pirates did get a look at him, he'd be different than they remembered. Of course, that increased the risk of detection by people on the *other* ship, who might have images of his real self for facial comparison, but he couldn't have everything. His display populated with information on the tender as Athena easily slid into the network. She said, "The codes are old, but they're UCCA."

Good, download whatever you can. While you're at it, find me somewhere to get weapons. Then, figure out where all these ships came from and where they're headed.

In a sarcastic growl, she replied, "You don't demand much, do you?" She addressed the first request immediately by highlighting the map on his display with a route leading to one of the many weapons and armor storerooms on the ship. It was logical that there would be so many, although he hadn't considered it in advance, since there would be ships in the field in need of replacements for human-sized weapons as well as the ship-sized ones.

He gathered a few strange looks at his helmet on the way, and he dealt with them by activating the suit's external speaker and saying in an embarrassed tone, "Malfunction. Heading to get it fixed." Suspicion turned to laughter in each case, and he reached his destination without being found out. The room held no guards, only rows of tall, locked cabinets. On his own, he would've had no chance of defeating their security with anything short of brute force. But with the AI integrated into the systems, the doors she thought he needed access to popped open one after the other.

The first contained a much-improved version of the EVA suit he wore, and he quickly stripped down and changed into it after setting the pristine helmet aside. It wasn't as good as his Special Forces jump suit, but it was only a few steps down from there. The next held an energy rifle that he slapped onto the magnetic hardpoints on his back. Projectile and energy pistols went into holsters attached to the thighs. Finally, he fastened the buckle of a utility belt covered with hardpoints and pouches and filled them with first-aid kits, emergency packs, and small explosives.

Now that he was fully re-equipped, he felt much better about life. It would be easy for him to impersonate a crew member, permitting him to move freely around the ship. *Athena, can you put my identity into their system so that if someone does scan me, they see something they'd expect?*

She replied, "Affirmative and done. It won't survive a deep investigation but should handle a superficial look."

Are you saying I'm superficial?

"Of course. Haven't I made that abundantly clear before?"

He shook his head. *So mean, as usual. Can you give me comms to the* Grace *without discovery?*

Her answer was the crackle of his system engaging and Cia's voice saying, "Twenty-five minutes out."

He nodded. "Good. Keep an ear on." *All right, what have you found out?*

"I've finished identifying the ships in the area, and you're going to find their origins very strange."

While you tell me, show me the path to some heavier munitions. Limpet mines, if they have them, or something similar. A plan was forming in his mind. The requested route illuminated on his display, and he tucked his new helmet under his arm with military precision and strode for the door. As he walked, the AI filled him in. "Each of the ships was officially listed as 'disappeared' or 'destroyed.' They're here under different names, of course, but the profiles and the drive signatures match the database I have. Fortunately, the Academy never deletes information, only adds to it. A modern Alliance database might have eliminated those records."

He frowned. *Why? It's data.*

"Secrecy. Efficiency. That sort of thing. Doubtless someone, somewhere along the line, thought getting rid of outdated and irrelevant ship profiles was a good idea."

He shrugged. *Yeah, that sounds like the military I know and love. Where did they get lost?*

"That's the most interesting part. All over the place. No clear pattern to it, and both the Alliance and the Confederacy sustained losses."

He shook his head slowly. *So what you're telling me is that someone, presumably Arlox or someone else within our government, has been cobbling together a secret fleet?*

"That would be my assessment, yes."

Damn. Well, that does explain the short staffing. If it's an off the books thing, then it wouldn't be that easy to rotate people in, at least not reliable people. You'd want to automate whatever you could.

She agreed. "That seems likely."

He reached the room where the explosives were stored and grinned. All the tools he was most familiar with lay right there in front of him like the treasure at the end of a map—limpet mines, the custom duffel backpack to carry them in EVA, and best of all, the heavy-duty grapnel gun that Special Forces soldiers used to deploy the explosives. *It's like Christmas and my birthday all wrapped into one.*

He loaded up a bag, considered his options for a moment, then grabbed another and filled it as well. Once he had a dozen of the mines, he stowed the rifle that had been across his back in yet another bag so no one would notice it and replaced it with the grapnel gun. *Connect me to the* Grace. When the channel sprang to life, he said, "Gonna light some candles in place of the original plan. Be ready to pick me up." He clicked off the mic. *Athena, any timetable on the pirate boarders' movements?* She had stayed connected to the pirate ship, which foolishly hadn't killed its wireless network.

"The ship should be out of here in fifteen minutes, and I think it's safe to assume they'll move soon after."

Do you have all the information we need?

"I do."

He nodded. *Perfect. Let's cause some trouble.*

CHAPTER NINETEEN

Jax climbed a maintenance ladder to the top of the ship and exited through a repair airlock. Athena had reviewed the schematics and decided that route offered the best combination of external positioning and detection avoidance. The pirate vessel he'd stowed away on was pulling out of the tube, a little below and to the left of his position, and angled upward as if it could read his desires and wanted to bring them to fruition. He aimed the grapnel gun at the craft and Athena placed a crosshair on his display to show him where it would hit. He informed her, "I'll accept whatever help you want to give me here, and for the duration of this adventure."

"Good that you asked, although I probably would've done it anyway."

He laughed. "I know. That's why I asked." He lined up the sights, felt the slight tremor as she adjusted his aim, and pulled the trigger. The gun contained a powerful set of magnets shaped like a dart at the end that trailed a long, thin, high-density cable. In this circumstance, making the shot required adjusting for distance, the tender's and the pirate ship's relative motion, and even the star's gravitational pull. He thought there was a chance he might have hit the target without Athena's help, but not a great one.

When the projectile opened and deployed its magnetic tines, they struck exactly where he'd aimed them and locked on. The winch was part of the gun, which was attached to his belt by a heavy carabiner. He pressed the button to activate the motor and let the rifle drop on its strap. His progress toward the other vessel was a little more awkward than he was accustomed to since instead of having only a backpack filled with six mines, which generally didn't interfere with balance, he carried another heavy bag in his hand that definitely did.

He landed on the side of the ship, activated his mag boots, made sure he had a good handhold, detached the grapnel from the hull, and reloaded it into the gun. Another advantage to Athena's presence in his head was that she possessed schematics of most ship types, which meant she could identify their weak points. On this pirate ship, that was a welded seam where two large, separately built sections joined. It was an economical shipbuilding method, but not a particularly high quality one, and it would work to his benefit. A mine positioned along it at the top of the ship could shatter the join and render the vessel inoperable. Two would make sure of it. He climbed up, placed both, and primed them to detonate at a trigger from either Athena or the *Grace*. She'd already transmitted the frequency back to his team. "Okay, where next?"

After the first jump, which they'd more or less planned, he'd known they would have to improvise based on the proximity of the other vessels. If it was him out there alone, he never would've been confident enough to pull it off and would already be signaling for a ride out of there. But an outline drew itself around one of the ships in his display, and a targeting mark glowed on it an instant later. He lifted the rifle and aimed it, felt Athena adjust his positioning again, and pulled the trigger. The grapnel flew true and landed precisely where it was supposed to.

This craft was an Alliance fighting ship, a small, older generation destroyer. It looked to have lost about half its armaments, and he wondered if someone had stolen it off the scrapheap after decommissioning or if it had disappeared during a battle. He figured there'd be time to sort out the details later. The weak point on this one was uncomfortably close to the engines, and he felt the vibration of the ship under his feet as he moved toward the vulnerable spot. When this mine went off, it would punch a hole in a place where a hole definitely shouldn't be, allowing the engines' output to escape in a direction the designers never intended. That would almost certainly render the ship unusable if the crew reacted quickly enough or potentially ram it into other ones nearby *and* render it useless if they didn't.

They repeated the process and sabotaged several vessels until Jax had only four mines left. He had his eye on one particular ship, the largest in the array, and asked Athena if they could reach it. She replied, "Not easily. How crazy are you feeling?"

He laughed. "About as much as usual, why?"

The AI looped Cia into the channel. "To accomplish it, the *Grace* will have to cross near us. We'll grapnel her, then use that momentum to swing out toward the other ship. You'll have to release and reel in the projectile, re-arm the weapon, and shoot it again, all in about fifteen seconds, or we'll overfly our mark and wind up tumbling off into space."

He shrugged. "Which isn't that big a deal since Cia will be able to pick us up if that happens."

The pilot snorted. "Hell, no. I'm going to blow this place up with you in it and enjoy every second of it."

Athena replied, "The problem is that we'll be moving fast enough that we might register on a ship's defensive computers. Defense cannons are nothing to take lightly."

Jax sobered. "Well, when you put it that way, let's not screw it up."

Cia questioned, "Are you sure you want to do this?"

He stood staring out of the collection of ships before him, counting them subconsciously. There were a lot. Dozens, some of them big enough that in a group they could easily threaten the *Cronus* and his people on board her, which he knew in his gut was where they were headed. "I think we have to give it a try. Cia, be ready to sweep around and pick us up or to put the *Grace* in the way of a cannon if it starts shooting at us. I presume that it wouldn't do too much damage."

"This isn't a warship, you know." An alarm blared in the background as she set the ship to combat readiness. "Try not to make it necessary, all right?"

"I'll do my best. Athena, lead us."

The AI gave commands to the pilot, who brought the *Grace* in. Again, the target illuminated in his display, and she helped him as he fired. The grapnel locked on and he was yanked from his feet and swung in the direction of the ship. Athena ordered, "Release." He hit the button on the rifle to kill the magnetic flow and triggered the motor to reel the projectile in. The dart folded back up as it returned, and he grabbed it and shoved it into the barrel to reset the firing mechanism. All the while he kept his eyes locked on what he was doing to avoid becoming disoriented by space whirling around him. She declared, "Target's up."

He saw the big ship farther away than he expected. Jax lifted the rifle and pointed it but was unable to keep it on the mark. He tried for several seconds, then stated, "Okay, Athena. It's all you. Trigger, too."

"Acknowledged. Lift your shoulders slightly." He complied and discovered that watching his arms move without his instruction was a rather surreal experience. The prosthetics lifted the weapon, pointed it at the ship, and pulled the trigger. It hit true, and less than a minute later he was on the vessel's upper hull. His display marked four points. He jogged to the nearest and secured one of the mines, then moved on to the next. He repeated the process until the mines were gone and the ship was decidedly in danger.

Without warning, six drones swarmed over the left side of the hull. Athena warned, "Down," and Jax dropped to the deck. Their initial blasts missed, and they circled for another approach. He pulled out his pistols and fired, taking two down in the first volley, then two more with the second. He sensed Athena's assistance, but it was a less intrusive, more natural feeling than it had been in the past. The remaining pair got off their shots, and he felt bullets rip through the material of his suit and dig into his torso.

He gasped at the pain and automatically dug for the pouch on the back of his right thigh that held patches. The bullet holes were small enough to be self-sealing, he realized once he took a second to look down at them, but the energy blast that had scored along his artificial left arm was not, and that's what was triggering the alarms in his helmet. Although the attack hadn't done any real damage, it had compromised the suit.

He slapped two patches on, then focused on the drones as they came around for another attack. He acquired the targets faster than he should've been able to, thanks to the assistance of the AI and the boost from the adrenaline she pumped through him, and the threats went down before they could shoot at him again. "Looks like they've discovered us. Cia, come get us." He pulled the grapnel gun off his back and ran in the direction of the ship.

The pilot replied, "On it."

Jax watched the *Grace* grow larger as it neared and hoped it would reach him before any other counterattack materialized. He fired the grapnel gun at the target Athena gave him, a couple of feet away from the side hatch and the airlock it secured, and the rifle pulled him in. As he approached, it became obvious that several ships were turning in their direction. They'd apparently noticed that a troublemaker was among them. "We can't wait, Athena. Blow it."

She cautioned, "Debris is a possibility. Shockwave, too."

"I know. But we've gotta do what we've gotta do. I'd rather not get shot down."

"Acknowledged."

The ships they'd mined went up all at once, explosions occurring along an uneven line. The extra damage he'd hoped for failed to materialize since all the crews shut down the disabled vessels quickly enough to avoid injuring the others. Jax laughed as he thought about the fact that he'd messed up the arrogant pirate captain's plans quite effectively. *That'll teach you to condescend to me, jerk.* He shook his head. "Okay, let me in, people. We need to talk to Stephenson and Maarsen right away. Our allies are in danger."

CHAPTER TWENTY

After a little time in the *Grace's* medical compartment getting various bruises and lacerations attended to, Jax and the crew gathered in the galley. The only one missing was Trianna, who was piloting the ship toward the nearest jump point. Their pursuers had fallen away to respond to the chaos of the exploding ships, leaving them safe to proceed.

He paced in a slow pattern, unable to still his motion. Cia stood, complaining that she spent enough time sitting down. That left the table for the other four members of his team. The AI's avatar occupied the display mounted on the wall. He requested, "Athena, please connect to Maarsen and Stephenson."

"Acknowledged." Informal conversation filled the minute or so it took for her to include the others, and when they were both present, Jax got straight to the point. "Thanks for joining us. Athena will bring you up to speed on what we discovered."

Her avatar shared the screen with the remote participants' faces. She informed everyone, "While on the tender, I was able to compromise their systems. Fortunately, their codes were old, and I had access to all of them. The pirate ships and the others in the system are planning to head to the Lorennsten system."

Stephenson cursed. "What a coincidence. So are we."

Jax nodded. "So, we can see what Arlox is thinking, anyway. He's finally going to make an overt strike against us, or more specifically against my Special Forces team and the *Cronus*."

The major shook her head. "Captain Jensen will be ticked."

He laughed at the mental image of the *Cronus*'s commander receiving the news. "That's quite an understatement. So, the question becomes, how do we think Arlox will play it?"

Maarsen advised, "We have to assume that Zavian has multiple plans in place. In his shoes, I would have one trap ready for the troops deploying to the planet, and another for the *Cronus* and whoever is with her."

Stephenson nodded. "Same here."

Cia shrugged. "It seems logical. But, for the sake of conversation, wouldn't it be more effective to attack the ship before the soldiers launched?"

Jax shook his head. "If the primary objective is to get my team, and secondarily to hit the *Cronus*, getting them away from her protection makes a lot of sense. That's the game in my opinion, based on the other attacks that have taken place on me and my allies." He thought again of Juno and hoped she was safe.

Maarsen chimed in, "I agree with Jackson. In any case,

it doesn't really matter. If we prepare for both and only one materializes, then we're still in good shape. If we only prepare for one, however, and two are in play," his words trailed off, and Jax was sure the others imagined the same dire consequences that he did.

Verrand asked, "Why is the bastard bothering with this little stuff anyway? Isn't he powerful enough to pretty much do what he wants without worrying about it?"

Stephenson replied, "Paranoia. The powerful are particularly susceptible to it."

Maarsen nodded. "Simply winning isn't sufficient for Zavian. He needs to eliminate his enemies in the process. Any victory is only half as sweet if threats still exist to endanger his desires."

Sirenno asked, "Major, could you cancel the mission? Or, you know, not show up?"

She shook her head. "He's got us boxed in on that one. Aside from the fact that it would be dereliction of duty and whoever was involved would wind up court-martialed, we'd also be leaving the people following us in without cover. We can't do that. We have a job to do, and despite whatever else is going on, it's a real job. Even if Arlox is messing about in our sandbox."

Jax asked, "Is the plan to deploy all three teams?"

His superior officer nodded. "Those are our instructions. We anticipate there will be fifteen or twenty times that number of enemies on the planet. There's no question that we need to set the battlefield ahead of time."

"What's your ETA?"

"Well, that's confidential, but I suppose I can share it with you all. Please promise not to tell the aliens when we're coming, though." A couple of laughs sounded in response, and she continued, "Two days. The main attack group will jump in about twelve hours after we go in and soften the place up."

He asked, "Do you have reconnaissance on the planet?"

"Funny you should ask that. No, we don't. All our satellites in the system have been knocked offline, and aside from the initial signals that the Confederacy base was under attack, there's been nothing else coming off the planet."

He nodded. "Jamming, probably. Another sign of Arlox's involvement."

Stephenson shrugged. "Or the aliens achieved victory quickly enough to preclude any more. There's always an outside chance that Arlox is simply taking advantage of something that was happening naturally anyway."

Maarsen shook his head. "I hate to argue with you, Anika, but this smacks of his style. There's no question in my mind that he's behind every piece of this."

Marshall said, "So what I'm hearing is that not only is this guy a total bastard, he's also a traitor."

Jax nodded. "Yep."

The other man growled, "Well then, we need to mess up his party, hard."

Jax couldn't have agreed more. "Here's what I think we should do. The *Grace* can deliver me to the planet, and I'll do a little work preparing the ground for the teams from the *Cronus*. I should at least be able to acquire enough intelligence to make sure they can overcome whatever surprises have been set for them. If I'm lucky, maybe I'll be able to turn some of those tricks back on the bad guys."

He looked up at the monitor again as he addressed his superior officer. "Then, when you deploy the teams, you send them down with heavier gear than usual. Normally, we want to be more flexible than deliberately overpowered," he explained to the others. "But in this case, adding in some heavy weapons might tilt the scales in our favor. As long as I'm there to check out the situation ahead of time, we can afford to sacrifice a little bit of flexibility for a lot more boom."

Everyone looked thoughtful, but no one replied. Finally, Stephenson broke the silence. "I can't say it's the smartest idea you've ever had, but it certainly sounds like the best one we're going to get. I sure as hell don't have anything better. Anyone else?"

Athena replied, "I believe this is the optimal path. And don't forget, with me along, Jax will have an improved chance of correctly assessing the situation that awaits your teams."

Stephenson nodded. "Yeah, I get that he's smarter with you in his head, but there's only so much you can improve on with the raw material available. And let's be honest, he's not exactly a brain trust to begin with." The familiar quirk at the corner of her lips brought a smile to his face.

Jax laughed. "I learned it from the best, Major. Just trying to emulate my superior officer." He waited until she opened her mouth to respond, and spoke quickly to interrupt her. "Anyway, I don't hear any arguments against, so I guess the question is, what assistance can the Academy and the *Cronus* offer us?"

Stephenson said, "My people will put together a care

package for you. Should help with your insertion into the planet."

"If they could coordinate the pickup with Cia, that would be perfect." Both women nodded. "Okay, now how much time do we have to play with?"

Athena replied, "Our best time to the system would be about eighteen hours. Depending on where we have to drop out to pick up the equipment the major mentioned, it will probably add another six to eight hours to our trip." The AI doubtless assumed the same thing Jax did, which was that the *Cronus* would already be nearing the system and would drop something off in reasonable proximity to it. Major Stephenson nodded, seemingly unconcerned.

He clapped his hands together. "All right then, we have a plan. Any last suggestions, Professor?"

Maarsen frowned. "You all try to stay safe. Remember that our enemy is strong, smart, and highly resourced. Don't take anything at face value. Like a chess grandmaster, he's always working multiple moves ahead."

Jax waved a careless arm at the screen. "He's met his match in Athena, trust me. She can out-think anyone in the universe."

In his mind, the AI observed, "That's an unlikely compliment."

Yeah, I'm trying to fill everyone with some confidence, so don't get too excited about it. I think we'll find ourselves challenged, but together we can overcome whatever we face. He clapped once. "Okay, people. Let's get this thing underway."

CHAPTER TWENTY-ONE

The *Grace* came out of jump long enough to secure the care package the *Cronus* had left behind for her and immediately jumped again, this time headed for her true destination. Jax reviewed the content of the crates, which included weapons, other gear, armor, and most exciting to him, a trio of jump suits. He joined the rest of the crew in the galley and shared the information with them.

Athena had taken over the monitor to use in her mission briefing, and one-third of it showed her avatar while the other two-thirds illustrated her points as she made them. "We're headed for the Lorrensten system, to planet Canian. The system has been in Confederacy hands for some time but is one the Alliance has kept an eye on, given its position on the border between our territories. It's also conveniently close to Alien Coalition space, ensuring that their interest in it could seem legitimate rather than the result of Arlox's action. Truly, it's an excellent location for a trap."

The image zoomed in from the system view to show

the second planet. "Until yesterday, this habitable world was in the hands of the Confederacy. Despite its prime spot, it was never substantially developed since all parties realized any significant construction would be an invitation for another faction to take it over. That outcome occurred most recently a day ago when the Alien Coalition invaded and eliminated the Confederacy troops on the planet. One message got out at the start of the battle announcing the attack. Since then, there have been no transmissions we're capable of detecting."

Kimmel asked, "Which means the signals aren't Confederacy, right? We wouldn't be able to detect the Coalition ones as easily?"

Athena replied, "Not necessarily. We've recorded and decoded various alien signals in the past. But we've discovered none on any of the expected frequencies. So, there could be a signal present we haven't previously encountered, but it's equally possible none have been sent." The computer expert nodded, and she continued, "The Confederacy did build a small installation during this ownership cycle, however." Beside her, the image zoomed in from the view of the entire planet as if it were a ship falling to the surface and stopped at an angle that showed the facility. "They appear to have borrowed from designs of the distant past and created a walled city."

Marshall nodded. "Not a terrible choice, as long as an attack came from the ground rather than the air. I think I'd probably have gone with a dome, myself."

Jax laughed. "Yeah, but domes have their flaws too, like the fact that a single EMP can ruin a defending force's day. No solution is perfect."

Athena continued, "The outer walls appear to be about twelve feet high and create a perfect square. There are gates to the north and south and a reinforced building in the center of the area. Outbuildings of various sizes surround it, purpose unknown."

Sirenno frowned. "You're saying we don't have past surveillance of this place?"

Jax shook his head. "Seems like any we did have was somehow erased from the system, according to Major Stephenson."

Cia snorted. "Arlox. Clever bastard."

Athena resumed speaking. "We presume the aliens will have compromised one or more of the walls in their efforts to take over the facility, and there hasn't been sufficient time to repair them. That should be considered a primary entrance route."

Jax nodded. "Even if they're whole, I shouldn't have too much of a problem climbing them, given the equipment the *Cronus* left me."

Athena finished, "Other than that, the only relevant information we have is about the surrounding countryside. It's a mix of trees and clearings, with neither roads nor paths cut into them."

Marshall asked, "So what's the plan?"

Jax stood tall from where he'd been leaning on the cabinets. "Originally, I'd thought the *Grace* would set down nearby and let me out to create some trouble. However, the fact that I have a jump suit and some Special Forces gear changes the situation dramatically. I'm going to jump from the ship from outside the atmosphere, then you all will descend somewhere they can't see you and find a nice place to hide. Close enough that you can come to the rescue, but far enough away that no one will notice you."

Cia interjected, "I think we can handle that."

He nodded. "So, the way this works is that the Special Forces deploy before the main assault to soften the place up. I'm going to extend that plan and go in before the Special Forces teams to see what Arlox has in store for them. I'll do my best to mess that up, which should give our people an advantage when they reach the ground."

Verrand asked, "What about the major's ship?"

"Yeah. We can't offer a lot on that score. Captain Jensen knows enemy ships will be coming, and we fed all the data we gathered on the ones in the tender's system to her. I suppose it's always possible the bad guys might step up their timetable, but they can't know we found that information. Athena owned their systems from the moment we were on board, and since the *Grace* was in disguise, there's no reason to suspect it was us. I think we'll be okay on that front. Unless one of you also has a hidden fleet lying around to bring to the party, I don't see that we could do much more than we have."

Cia felt all the eyes in the room turn to her and scowled. "What? Yes, my family has a lot of ships, but trade vessels lack a certain offensive capability if you know what I mean."

Jax laughed. "I think what will happen is the *Cronus* will send out a message telling the rest of the fleet not to jump in if she gets in trouble, or at least warning them of the changed situation. If the captain is smart, and I know she is, she has a plan for how she'll retrieve her troops and get to a jump point if things go wrong."

Marshall nodded thoughtfully. "I noticed that all along you've said 'I,' when there are three jump suits."

The others made murmurs of agreement. Verrand observed, "And we've all already proved we're pretty good in a fight."

Jax shook his head. "I have to do this alone. This isn't your battle. We're taking on alien soldiers, likely elite ones. It requires a level of skill that no one outside the military is going to possess. I have nothing but the greatest respect for you all and would take you into just about any situation, but this is one where experience will make a serious difference. Potentially, literally a life-and-death difference."

Cia added, "Besides, we'll be nearby to help out. That said, Jax, you're being an idiot again."

On the monitor, Athena's avatar burst out in laughter. "Oh, good. I thought I would have to be the one to tell him."

He turned so he could scowl at them both simultaneously. "I presume there's more you'd like to say?"

Cia tilted her head toward the avatar on the screen. "Go ahead."

Athena countered, "Oh no, you, please. I'll have ample opportunity to remind him of what an idiot he is when we're on the planet."

The pilot laughed. "Okay. Remember back when we first met, and you were a control freak who had problems with trusting other people?"

Jax didn't appreciate the sudden turn in the conversation, not one bit. "Yeah, I seem to recall something like that."

She nodded. "Well, it seems as if you didn't learn your

lesson. You have another person right here in our crew who was in the military and offers the ability to double your potential effectiveness by taking him along with you. Instead, you're thinking of yourself as the lone hero again."

He sighed. "First of all, I think you're oversimplifying my alleged personality issues."

Athena interjected, "Oh, definitely not alleged."

Cia piled on, "And we're only scratching the surface of your personality problems. But please, do continue."

Despite the situation's seriousness, the people around the table were smiling to one degree or another, except for Marshall, who intensely stared at him. Jax continued, "You know, jump suits are a Special Forces thing. Correct me if I'm wrong Kenton, but you've probably never used one."

The other man leaned back in his chair, shook his head, and spread his hands in a gesture of defeat. "You're right. It's true; I haven't. If only there were some way to help me with that part of it. Like, I don't know, maybe a state-of-the-art, only-one-in-the-universe, artificial intelligence with the ability to transmit instructions over short distances using some sort of, like, comm system. I realize it's crazy, but I think if we had those ridiculously hard to get things, it just might work."

Everyone else burst into laughter as Jax shook his head resignedly. "You realize how risky this is, right? Everything we've done up to now is completely unlike going up against an entrenched enemy."

Marshall nodded. "But you're not planning on taking them on toe-to-toe, right? We're talking about subtle moves, subterfuge, that sort of thing."

"You have a point, and I can't argue the fact that it could

turn out having both of us there would be better than me alone. But it's a severe risk."

"You've made that clear. Let me ease your conscience. I understand this is incredibly dangerous and nonetheless, I choose to come along. Because I believe I can help. I guarantee you that anyone else here if they had military training, would step up and take the third suit."

Every member of his team bobbed their heads, and Jax found himself moved by their commitment and trust. "Okay, then. Marshall and I will jump. That means the *Grace* has a little more free agency than I thought. Cia, what do you think you can do?"

She considered it for a moment before replying. "We have the mining drones. We can use them as repeaters to keep our comms secure. It's a lot harder to detect the signals when they're bouncing place to place than when they're going out everywhere."

"Athena, can you hack the software in the drones to make that work?"

"Count on it."

He nodded. Line-of-sight communications were almost impossible to mess with. "You'll set down far enough away that the ship won't be at risk? I can't stress how important it is that the *Grace* is available as a safety net in case something goes wrong."

Cia answered, "You know it."

Jax shook his head one final time. "Marshall, you're a crazy man. Last chance to make the smarter choice."

The other man shrugged. "I know. But, at the end of the day, I'm going to look really good for having done this."

Everyone laughed, and Jax sighed with a smile. "You

wouldn't have thought I could find a bunch of people crazier than I am, but here you all are."

Athena added, "Smarter, too. Don't forget smarter."

Jax rolled his eyes. "Anyone want to take her off my hands? Er, out of my head?"

Kimmel pointed out, "Haven't we concluded doing that would kill you?"

He nodded. "Yeah, but at the moment, that's starting to sound like a desirable alternative."

CHAPTER TWENTY-TWO

When the *Grace* entered the Lorennsten system, it was again on the outskirts to ensure she would remain undetected. Jax, already in his jump suit, watched from his customary position between the pilots. Cia observed, "No sign of alien ships."

"Any chance that they're cloaked or something?"

Trianna snorted. "There's always a chance of everything when you come right down to it, isn't there?"

Cia shook her head. "She's right, anything's possible, but it's unlikely. Certainly we don't know what every ship has, especially where the aliens are concerned, but I would think that if they'd created reliable cloaking technology, we'd have heard about it. Either from the Academy or the military. I think we're okay."

"Surveillance satellites or other tech around the planet?"

"None that I can see. Seems like they smacked the Confederacy off the world and left town."

It was weird enough to be concerning. "All the better to

make it seem like an irresistible opportunity, I guess. Okay. We stick with the plan. I'll grab Marshall and get ready."

Cia kicked the engines to maximum, and the starfield moved on the display. "Have a good flight."

He shook his head as he left the compartment. "Somehow, I don't think there's going to be anything good about this experience."

They'd decided to use the side hatch airlock and leap from beyond the atmosphere, in case the aliens on the ground did have some detection in place despite their inability to find any. The plan called for the *Grace* to remain as unnoticed as possible, and while he wasn't relying on the ship not being spotted on the way in, he certainly hoped for it. Cia had plans and ideas to deal with a potential sighting, if necessary, and he trusted her to handle it. He found Marshall waiting in the airlock with their gear and laughed. "You're eager to get going too, I see."

The other man smiled a little, but his tension was obvious. "Sooner started is sooner finished, right?"

"Absolutely, although this will be like a lot of military missions and include a big hurry up and wait component. Once we set things up, we'll still need to delay until our backup arrives to get the ball rolling."

"Still."

Jax nodded. "Yeah. Let's get into the gear and run through our final checks. I'm guessing we still have about thirty minutes before we're in place, but no reason to delay."

They spent the excess time going through jump procedures. Jax tried to give the other man the broad strokes of several months' worth of training in case Athena lost connection with his suit during the maneuver. In truth, the gear would take care of the safe landing part of the jump, which was doubtless Marshall's biggest concern. It was the steering beforehand that required some skill and potentially overriding the chute deployment for a moment or two in order to land where they intended. Jax had picked out a clearing about a mile away from the installation as their target but had warned his partner it could change on the way down since they had no clear intel on what defenses the aliens might have put in place while they had no eyes on them.

Marshall offered a lot of affirmative responses, clearly invested in making sure Jax knew he was completely ready. When Cia gave them the five-minute warning, Jax still felt conflicted about the other man's involvement. He reminded himself, *His choice. Not mine.*

Athena replied, "Exactly. You'd do well to remember that, whatever happens."

Easier said than done. He announced, "All right. Let's switch to internal air supply." His partner complied, and the readout in Jax's display, which included command functions, showed that the other man's equipment was operating properly. He hit the button to evacuate the atmosphere inside the airlock, then called, "Cia, please open the side hatch. We're ready to go."

The pilot confirmed, "Affirmative," and the door slid aside. The sight of the planet below filled the opening. She'd angled the *Grace* to ensure they faced it for their maneuver. Jax looked down at the green world below. "Last chance."

Marshall replied, "Shut it. Let's jump."

"You first." Jax following after had been the plan all along. Marshall threw himself out of the airlock, pushing off toward the sphere below like a skier launching himself out of a gate. Jax jumped a couple of seconds later to ensure they wouldn't smash into each other, then announced, "We're clear. Seal it up and stay safe."

Cia's voice was full of concern. "Same to you, jerkwad. *Grace* out."

The first several minutes of the fall were serene, almost relaxing. Their ride got a little rougher when they hit the thicker part of the atmosphere and resistance began in earnest. He heard Marshall grunting as he was buffeted during the passage, but there was no panic or alarm in it. Jax nodded in respect of the man's toughness and ordered, "Athena, show us the way."

A yellow line that curved as it neared the planet appeared in their displays. It included waypoints demonstrating where they should let the flight suit portion of their outfit catch the air to direct them on the correct heading and where they should deploy their parachutes. Marshall would see only one route, but Jax had both in his helmet, along with a telltale that would warn him if his partner exceeded a certain distance beyond his marks. He grinned at the joy of being airborne, as he usually did at this point in a jump. *Gotta live in the moments between*, he thought to himself. "All right, here we go. Not much I can do to help you from here on out. Follow the instructions and try not to hit me when you land, or we're going to have words."

The other man laughed. "Roger."

Both flew through the proper markers along the way, and while Marshall did take a tumble during the landing instead of ending the jump in a clean jog like Jax did, all in all, it was a solid effort. Jax pulled off his helmet and gathered in his parachute, speaking each part of the process aloud to keep Marshall up to speed. It took less than ten minutes for them to strip off their suits, pull out the gear that had ridden down in their backpacks and strap it on over armor and uniforms, and rig the jump suits to explode if anyone without the appropriate UCCA transponder tried to mess with them.

Tall trees with thin trunks and large forking branches filled with needles surrounded the clearing he'd chosen as their landing zone. His intended path to their destination went through more trees since he'd decided to approach from the most densely wooded side. The images the *Grace* had acquired during the runup to the jump had confirmed it was the best choice, both because it was hidden and because it was the option closest to the target.

He would have selected differently if aliens were watching, but they'd seen no evidence of any activity at all. Not one creature moved in or around the installation. That was worrisome, but since he was already mentally prepared for traps and dangers, it didn't rise to the level of a significant deterrent. If he were with the Special Forces team and dropping onto the planet in such a situation, he would've been far more alarmed. But Jax and his allies already knew there was a double-, triple-, or quadruple-cross in play, so he'd have to stay on his toes and deal with whatever trouble lay ahead when he reached it.

He led the way forward with his rifle held close to his chest to avoid snagging it on the ubiquitous branches. They'd chosen energy for the primary weapon since more of the alien races they knew about were armored against physical damage than were against energy damage. Each also wore a stun pistol on one hip, in case the electric taser option would work better, and a heavy projectile pistol on the other, filled with explosive rounds in case brute force was the best option. He also carried extra magazines, a medkit, and an advanced sensor module that would give him the ability to see trouble coming from an extended range, plus an extra battery to power the sensor.

It was a heavy assortment, and again his legs complained about the fact that he'd been spending less time than usual in the gym. He ignored it, determined not to show any sign of weakness in front of Marshall. The latter walked along behind him without complaint, identically outfitted except for the additional sensor and battery. The other man asked, "Any new information?"

He shook his head. "The communication relays aren't up yet, right, Athena?"

She replied, "Correct. The *Grace* has to set down before releasing the drones."

"And whatever else is in those other two pods?"

The AI laughed. "Wouldn't you like to know?"

His voice turned serious. "If it has any bearing on the mission we're on right now, I need to know."

The playful tone left hers. "One is filled with explosive devices. I don't have access to the Rearden company inventory to know what kind. The other contains a ship-to-ship missile."

He nodded. "Thanks. Especially since you probably

could've made the argument that I still didn't need to know."

"Cia's surprises aren't worth additional danger. But if you could act like you don't know anything about them when she reveals them, I would appreciate it."

He chuckled. "Gotcha."

Marshall, who had stared at him throughout the exchange, remarked, "You two have the weirdest partnership I've ever seen."

Athena snorted. "You should try it from in here."

Jax nodded. "If I die and someone offers you the opportunity to have her implanted in your brain, I suggest you pass."

The other man made a face. "Eww. That kind of presumes I'll have to cut off your head and take it with me if something goes wrong. I'm not normally squeamish, but I don't really enjoy the idea of carrying around a severed skull, either."

Jax laughed. "You said you wanted to come along, remember? Okay, radio silence, nothing but essential talking from here on out. We'll use hand signals." The other man nodded, and as they reached the edge of the tree line, Jax crouched to review the scene ahead of them. The wall had taken a lot of damage during the aliens' assault, leaving a gaping hole three feet wide at the bottom that expanded upward in a V. Beyond it lay the outbuildings that Athena had described, and the reinforced fortress structure rose to three stories in the center of the complex. *For a walled city, it's pretty small.*

Athena replied, "It's not like they intended to have a

civilian population inside it. That was simply the best metaphor at the time."

Any signals? Security systems?

"None active."

Give me thermal. The sensor package switched into the requested mode, and the display in his glasses rendered shapes in yellows, oranges, blues, and greys. There was no sign of any individual body heat signatures, although each of the buildings glowed with warmth. The overall climate was fairly balmy so the effect could be due to heat absorption.

That's weird. Think they're shielded?

Athena replied, "It's the most likely explanation. A defensive facility would benefit from such a choice."

Let's try electrical.

The image switched so that anything with an electrical charge to it glowed. All the buildings did, and the center fortress was triple the intensity of the others. No clear evidence of life was visible on that scan, either.

Jax sighed. *So, we have no idea what we're getting into is what you're saying.*

Athena replied, "I'm not saying anything, so you must be talking to yourself this time. One of the early signs of insanity, you know." He shook his head and turned toward Marshall, who had waited patiently and quietly. He pointed at himself, then at his partner, and indicated the facility. The other man nodded his understanding.

Guess we're going to have to do it the hard way and rely on visuals. Time to take a walk.

CHAPTER TWENTY-THREE

Jax led the way through the breached wall with Marshall trailing close behind him. He stayed low and peered in both directions before crossing the gap, in case there were aliens nearby that for some reason he couldn't see with the sensors. But nothing waited for them. No sign of movement, no activity. *This is really weird.*

Athena replied, "Agreed."

He used hand signals to indicate to Marshall what they were going to do next, then dashed for the nearest outbuilding and set his back against the wall. His partner followed a step behind and took a position at his left. *Athena, any way you can boost my sensors?*

"Standby." His glasses showed the electrical scan again, and this time the colors were more intense, but it revealed no additional information. When she switched to the thermal mode, a flicker encroached on the edge of his vision. He turned his head and saw heat sources on the opposite side of the wall. They were horizontal as if they were in bunks or something. *Maybe they're nocturnal?*

Athena replied, "Could be. There are a significant number of alien races in our records that are indeed nocturnal."

He put his mouth next to Marshall's ear. "This is beyond strange. But there are heat signatures in the building. It looks like a lot of them, and they're sleeping." His partner nodded and sketched a question mark in the air. Jax shrugged. "If there are some in each building, then trying to get in and cause trouble is almost certainly a bad idea. And if they're in this one, they're probably in the others. I say we put explosives on the doors, so when they come out, *boom*." Marshall nodded again.

Athena asked, "And if someone should come out before we want them to?"

He shrugged. *We run. If you have a better plan, I'm ready to hear it.* No response was forthcoming. He handed his rifle to Marshall, pulled the pack from his back, and dug in it for the explosives. They were smaller versions of the limpet mines he'd used on the ships and could be set to detonate by remote trigger or movement, making them useful in a wide variety of situations. He crept around to the first building's door with his partner a step behind traversing his weapon in a pattern that covered all approaches.

Jax knelt and attached the mine to the door near the handle. When the portal opened inward, the device would read the motion and explode. It stood out against the barrier's light-colored plastic but would only look like a palm-sized dark splotch from a distance. *And if we see someone wandering around once everything's trapped up, we shoot them. No problem there.*

They mined each of the outbuildings, carefully moving from cover to cover, eating up much more time than Jax would've preferred. He sensed the same frustration in his partner's expression. A couple of hours had passed when they finished, which meant the Special Forces team wasn't all that far out. *Athena, anything from the* Grace?

"The communication drones are in place, but nothing more than the channel's existence. They're remaining silent."

Good call, I guess. He put his mouth next to Marshall's ear again. "How about we take a look at the main building?" He slung the backpack over his shoulders, accepted the return of his rifle, and led the way toward the structure. Like the other structures, this one had no windows to offer insight as to what lay within. Electrical scanning displayed significant activity everywhere, and thermal scanning showed several figures, seemingly sleeping. He shook his head. *I certainly expected to find something going on in here, at least.*

Athena replied, "It wouldn't be much of a trap if you got what you expected, would it?"

Fair point. Heh. Wouldn't Arlox lose his mind if he knew that I was right here messing with a trap he'd set for other people?

"Maybe you can tell him at some point."

Probably not. I find it difficult to believe we'll take that one alive. I bet his subordinates want to kill him as much as any of us do. He walked around the entire perimeter of the building and placed mines on both doors he discovered. Then he retreated to the tree line to wait for what was to come.

As he settled down beside him, Marshall asked, "Did that seem too easy to you?"

Jax nodded. "Definitely. Something is going on here, and I have no idea what it is. Let's hope they didn't account for our early entry and love of things that go boom."

The other man laughed. "Let's hope. I'll drink to that." They both downed some ration bars and water, refreshing themselves as Athena kept a countdown running for the Special Forces teams' arrival.

About fifteen minutes before they'd expected the team to be on the ground, she said, "I'm reading Special Forces transponders on the way down. Twelve of them. They are relaying through our repeaters."

Jax nodded. The plan had been to use the drones for contact with the ships in orbit to keep that connection secure as well, at least until the squads linked up with him and Marshall. Likely the transponders were feeding back to the *Cronus*, and her crew was sending that data down through the transmitters. "Excellent. So, we wait for them to get here, and we attack the place together."

He watched in his display glasses as the little dots got bigger and bigger, then landed in a clearing about a mile away from the opposite side of the installation. He nudged Marshall. "Let's circle to meet them." When they'd covered about half the distance to the other tree line, something he hadn't noticed previously caught his eye and he froze in place to examine it. "Athena, was that antenna there before?" A stubby piece of metal showed on top of the central fortress, and he didn't recall seeing it during their recon or in any of the photos he'd studied.

"Negative."

"Okay, so something in the facility apparently woke up. I don't like anything about that. I think we should detonate the explosives ourselves. What's your opinion?"

The other man replied, "They're not big enough to bring down the structures and will probably do far less damage than if we waited since the aliens won't be right next to them."

Jax nodded. "Unless our enemies have something different in mind and don't plan to use the doors in the first place." He made the decision. "Athena, blow the explosives."

She didn't reply, but a string of staccato detonations occurred within the compound. The door of the nearest outbuilding turned into shrapnel that flew inside. He expected to see aliens boiling out of it, wounded and angry, and was confused when they didn't. His confusion lasted only a moment before the entire facility went up in a mammoth blast that knocked him and Marshall flying. He landed on his back six feet from where he'd stood and tumbled backward as the shockwave tossed him around. When he stopped, he observed, "Bloody hell, that wasn't us."

Athena replied, "No, it wasn't. Someone wired the compound to explode. Apparently, the smaller charges were enough to trigger it."

He got up, ran in the direction of the Special Forces teams, and activated his comm connection. "Wasp, this is Axe. The facility blew up."

Beatrice O'Leary's voice came back to him, and he realized it had been some time since he'd heard it and that he'd missed it. "Roger, Axe, we noticed. What's your status?

"Heading toward you as fast as we can."

"Affirmative." There was chatter over the comm from voices he didn't recognize. With a note of concern, she added, "Run faster, Axe. The *Cronus* is reporting movement not too far from us. A lot of movement."

Jax and Marshall burst into the clearing where the Special Forces soldiers stood guard in a ring with their rifles trained outward. The transponders in their uniforms ensured they'd show as friends on their allies' displays, but running toward the weapons was still at least momentarily alarming. Jax traded hellos with the captains of the other two units but ran over and bumped fists with everyone in his, then grabbed Beatrice O'Leary's forearm and held it a little longer than necessary. It felt incredibly good to see them again.

He realized he wasn't including Marshall and introduced his Academy partner to the rest of the team. They exchanged nods, handshakes, and fist bumps. O'Leary said on a private channel, "Command's yours if you want it, boss."

He shook his head. "Your team, your show. Tell us what you need us to do."

She grinned and called, "Dare, get these two some real weapons." The big man handed over a pair of heavy rifles, each of which was more than double the firepower of the ones they carried even before you included the grenade launcher slung underneath. Bandoliers of grenades flew through the air toward them next, and they both caught them cleanly. They put on the equipment, surrendered their old rifles, and Jax took a moment to ask Marshall, "You good?"

The other man nodded. He had an energetic look Jax recognized from so many previous missions. He clapped Marshall on the shoulder. "You'll do great. You're on my six unless Wasp tells you differently." Jax walked back over to O'Leary. "So, what's the plan here?"

She gave a dramatic sigh. "Well, we *were* going to take over the facility and use it as a defensive position to wipe the aliens off the planet. But then, you know, you guys blew up our objective."

The others on the channel laughed, and Jax shook his head. "Technically, that wasn't my fault."

O'Leary snorted. "Axe, you're among people who know you. Please. No need to lie." He rolled his eyes.

Athena enthused, "I'd forgotten how much I enjoy it when you're with Acting Captain O'Leary."

Shut it. "And now?"

She shrugged. "Take down as many aliens as we can since the installation isn't relevant anymore. We have to keep them busy until our backup arrives to bail us out."

"When will that be?"

"Major Stephenson advanced the timetable. Two hours tops."

He nodded. "Good for her. Smart as the day is long."

Sparks called, "Boss, you might want to take a look at this."

O'Leary crossed to where the man stood in front of a heavy sensor module that had dropped with the team. On its display was a semi-circle of heat signatures closing on their position. "That's not looking too good."

The other captains, Catherine Lorenzo and Hugo Frangilo, showed up a moment later. The woman asked, "What's not good?"

O'Leary pointed. "There's a lot more of them than we expected from the *Cronus*'s warning. What is that, a hundred or so?"

Sparks nodded. "At least. There might be more behind them. Now and again I see a ghost image back there."

O'Leary asked, "The drones have anything to offer?"

He shook his head. "They went up, and we lost contact before they saw anything. They must have some sort of defense bot up there."

Jax and O'Leary breathed, "Dammit," at the same moment, and he gave a small laugh. "Tell me we're going to go with the prudent choice and get the hell out of here."

She looked at the other two squad leaders. "That sounds like a good idea to me. There's no way our twelve can take down their hundred, even with the heavier gear."

"Fourteen," Jax corrected, which earned a scowl from O'Leary.

Lorenzo said, "Slow retreat, we leapfrog back and cover each other. Eventually, we'll probably have contact, but we don't want to run all out and suddenly discover there's more of them waiting behind us."

O'Leary nodded. "Sounds good. What direction?"

Jax interrupted, "Wait one on that." *Athena, connect me to the* Grace, *please.*

"Go ahead."

"Cia, where are you?"

She replied instantly by giving him the coordinates. He passed them on to O'Leary and told her, "I brought a ride. We can all fit."

She laughed. "I knew there'd eventually be a reason for me to miss you. Turns out it took an alien ambush to make it happen." Her voice switched into command mode as she yelled, "All right people, let's move. The aliens are coming, and we need to not be here when they arrive."

Their team was the first to surrender their position, running at the fastest pace they could sustain for a third of a mile before turning back and pointing their weapons forward. The next group passed them, and the last did as well. When it was almost their turn to run again, Marshall hissed, "Contact." Jax spotted the movement in the trees a hundred feet or so away that had alarmed his partner.

O'Leary's voice was calm as she ordered, "Everyone, grenades, incendiary, on my mark." Jax found the right ammunition by touch and inserted the canister into the launcher, then aimed straight ahead and slightly up. When she gave the word, six soft belches heralded the grenades arcing toward their enemies, and before the munitions landed the team had already turned to run. The forest behind them went up in an explosion of sound and flame, and O'Leary reported the contact to the rest of the Special Forces troops as they jogged forward.

They stopped a full mile later, listening as the other teams used the same strategy to deter their pursuers. On the squad channel, Jax asked, "They won't be stupid enough to do that again, will they?"

O'Leary replied, "It sure would be nice to think so, but if I were them, I'd move to flank us."

He nodded. "Yeah, I had the same thought."

She blew out a loud breath. "Any chance of getting that ship closer? This is getting a little hairier than I expected."

Athena relayed the question, and Cia replied in the affirmative. Another clearing lit up on his map, one about a mile and a half away. He shared it with the others, and the leaders conferred briefly before agreeing it made sense to do it. They changed their approach, deciding that the back two teams would race for the extraction point. At the same time, O'Leary's squad, now unfortunately in the front position, would retreat more slowly and attempt to delay the enemy before turning and running when the ship was nearby. Jax didn't love the plan, but he didn't have a better idea either, beyond the leapfrogging. And keeping the aliens away from the *Grace* sounded pretty good to him.

A flicker of motion ahead and to his right caused him to snap his rifle up and pull the trigger, and an alien screamed as it fell. O'Leary ordered, "Retreat by twos. Dare and Books first, Axe and Marshall second. Me, Strings, and Einstein third. One hundred yards, then stop and wait for the next." The enemy seemed to know that their quarry was slipping out of their hands, and they advanced aggressively, taking loss after loss to the Special Forces soldiers' rifles and grenades without slowing.

O'Leary growled, "Okay, screw this. Grenades, then run." They complied and dashed for where the *Grace* would soon be. It became quickly apparent that they might lose the foot race, and Jax had a moment of worry about it before he heard Cia's whooping cry as the ship flashed by over their heads. Behind them, a series of explosions went off that in aggregate sounded almost as loud as the one that blew up the installation, and caused him and the rest of the team to stumble. They made it to the *Grace* without further problems. The ship landed as they arrived, and he collapsed on the deck as they lifted off. *Explosives, huh?*

Athena replied, "In a pod, explosives, yes."

You didn't mention they were quite that powerful.

"As I said, I was unable to access the inventory, so I didn't know."

He shook his head. *Why don't I believe you?*

She laughed. "Would I lie to you?"

He pushed himself up off the floor and headed forward to have a word with the pilot. *You might, Athena. You might.*

CHAPTER TWENTY-FOUR

The *Grace* blasted out of the atmosphere into the formerly empty space surrounding the contested world where the *Cronus* was in the middle of a battle. Many of the ships they'd seen in the tender's system were involved, the ones they hadn't wrecked, anyway. But probably much to their enemies' surprise given their ahead-of-schedule arrival, so were several Alliance ships. Jax, his team, and the Special Forces soldiers watched on the galley's display, most of them sitting on the floor. O'Leary said, "Captain Jensen had a good plan. Once we jumped out of the shuttles, she was going to use them as missiles to take out some enemies."

Lyton laughed. "Yeah, being packed in there with all of those explosives and automated piloting wasn't a great time, let me tell you." The *Grace* continued to the nearest jump point, then leapt into the system where they'd agreed to meet up with the *Cronus* after she fought free. She arrived about an hour later, and everyone except Trianna transferred over to the bigger ship.

As soon as they were on board, a person in the uniform of a *Cronus* crew member took them in hand and led them to one of the large briefing rooms Major Stephenson used when she needed to talk to all her subordinates at once. She was pacing on a low stage at the front of the chamber. The galley had provided sandwiches and drinks on a table along one wall, and they dug in, carrying the food to their seats while his superior officer stood impatiently watching. When they were all seated, she began, "While you all were playing games with the aliens down on the planet, the Academy was working hard on figuring out Arlox's movements. They found something."

Excitement thrilled through Jax. *Finally, a solid lead on the bastard.*

Athena cautioned, "Don't get your hopes up. We thought we had him nailed down a couple of other times. As I recalled, those ended in you getting injured."

Shut it. He asked, "What did they discover?"

Stephenson scowled. "Not sure. Professor Maarsen wants to tell us all at once. Flair for the dramatic and all." She hit a button, and the large display at the front of the room came to life to show the Academy leader's face. He wasn't smiling and wasn't scowling, but definitely occupied a point somewhere on the "not happy" part of the continuum. He began, "Those of you who haven't been working closely with us are probably unaware that we've planted a tracking agent of a sort on some of Zavian Arlox's people. A bunch of them were present for a substantial amount of time on a Confederacy planet of interest to us, and they suddenly shifted location today. Naturally, we were curious about why they might have done so. So, we sent in our best technology to take a look."

His face disappeared from the display, and the image of a planet with several moons appeared on it. "This is the Wokoth system, planet Rill."

Marshall interjected, "What's there that's worth caring about?"

Maarsen's voice had a hint of his teacherly persona in it. "On the planet itself, nothing. However, it appears that our friends in the Intelligence Division have constructed a base on one of its moons." The image zoomed in a little to show the outlines of the facility, but it lacked detail.

Cia asked, "Can you go in further?"

Maarsen's shaking head returned to the screen. "We can't. To avoid detection, we're leaving our drone right where it is."

O'Leary prompted, "So why is this place interesting, other than the fact that it's a probably super-secret, off-the-books Intelligence Division base?"

Maarsen chuckled at her description. "There's been a lot of chatter going back and forth from that very remote base. I've called in some of our most valuable resources to examine the signals, likely removing their usefulness as assets ever again. But they're the best cryptologists we have, with access to the most recent Alliance codes. No one positioned in the Intelligence Division, unfortunately, but our data provided enough of a baseline for them to crack the encoded transmissions. There is a meeting happening there quite soon, and Arlox will be there in person for it."

A ripple of anticipation ran through everyone in the room. Cia hissed, "Yes," and several others echoed her.

Jax said, "So, the plan is to blast the moon to dust with him on it, right? Use the *Cronus* to pummel the installation into tiny pieces of nothingness?"

Stephenson scowled. "Try not to be stupid, Jackson. There's no way an Alliance warship can openly attack an Alliance base. If we survived whatever effort they made to capture us afterward, we'd live only long enough for them to court-martial us, *then* shoot us."

Venn suggested, "How about we hit him on his way in? Do we know what ship he'll be on?"

Maarsen shrugged. "We could find out, but that approach has the same problem. The *Cronus* can't take official action."

Jax growled, "You wouldn't have brought us this far without a solution in mind, Professor. Let's have it."

He chuckled. "You're correct. We've been working the situation from all angles. The only viable option seems to be getting a small team inside the installation before they realize the base is compromised. And the only way to do that is to arrive on a ship that they expect to see. My people tell me that we have to assume they'll shoot first and ask questions later if faced with any vessels they don't recognize."

Stephenson nodded. "From what we know of Arlox, he's a believer in the power of double-crosses, which means he'll be extremely paranoid about someone doing the same to him. There's no way he or his people would trust an unknown ship."

Jax sighed. "Well, that seems like a pretty big ask."

Maarsen shook his head. "Not as big as you think. It

turns out that someone you're familiar with arrived late to the meetings on Earth and stayed behind when the rest departed. He'll take a separate Intelligence Division ship to the meeting if the information our agent at the government center in Tokyo acquired is correct."

Jax laughed. "Seems like our friend Quentin is having a tough month."

Chuckles traveled around the room, and Maarsen nodded. "We'd noticed the ship was in orbit and had thought it was there for Arlox. That was his clever move, leaving ahead of time while we were busy watching the ship." He shook his head. "There's no denying that he's a smart man. Nonetheless, we have a ship, and on it a person who needs to get to that same meeting, by all accounts. So, this gives us an opportunity."

Jax asked, "I guess we need to hoof it to Earth so we can capture his ride before it leaves?"

Stephenson shook her head. "Impossible. The timeframe doesn't work."

Maarsen continued, "We've got that covered. I was able to activate one of our alumni who works in engineering at the shipyard that built the craft. They created a backdoor in the computer systems for maintenance purposes, as you'd expect. She believes it's probably still active. If she's correct, we can exploit it."

Verrand laughed. "Too bad Arlox wasn't on that ship. We could've simply set it to self-destruct, called the thing done, and gone out for victory drinks."

Maarsen nodded. "But then we'd lose the opportunity to discover what this meeting is all about, and something tells me it will probably turn out to be important knowledge to have. In any case, we'll instruct the ship to divert from its course, drop out of jump, and go dark at a certain location. When it does, you'll be there to take control of it. That should make it possible for you to break into the installation quietly."

Cia asked, "What's to keep them from calling for help once they get the power back up?"

Stephenson replied, "I've got that covered. We're going to replace one of your expended pods with a heavy-duty jammer. You should be able to ensure that no signal gets in or out."

She scowled. "And turn the *Grace* into a target while we do it."

"We're not in a safe business. Risks abound."

Jax nodded. "Okay, so you've given us the good news. That leaves the bad. What is it?"

Stephenson chuckled. "How like you to be a pessimist, Jackson."

"Uh-huh. Nice deflection. Are you going to answer my question or keep acting like a bureaucrat?"

She scowled at the insult. "I can only release one squad to accompany you. The other two need to stay with the *Cronus* and get back to the planet we just left. We still have our original mission, and they'll be expecting us back shortly to finish it."

Jax twisted to face the other members of his Academy team. "I know this is a stupid question, but is there any chance I can get you all *not* to come along and instead stay here on the *Cronus* where it's comparatively safe?"

They all shook their heads at him. Cia also rolled her eyes and added, "Yep, you're still an idiot."

"Okay. Then I guess we're all in. Speaking for myself, I'm very much looking forward to seeing our friend Quentin again."

CHAPTER TWENTY-FIVE

Before the *Cronus* departed, Major Stephenson arranged for all the possible toys the teams could need to be transported to the *Grace*. Jax had rarely been so happy to see his familiar equipment arrayed and awaiting his selection. Although the materials the Academy provided had been sufficient thus far, it simply wasn't up to Special Forces standards. He looked forward to having his tried-and-true gear to rely on for the mission ahead.

The teams had meshed effectively with none of the "One group over here and the other group over there" nonsense that sometimes plagued combinations like this. Instead, everyone had gathered in the cargo compartment to dig through the supplies and outfit themselves for the assault. They compared preferences and made choices that would complement the selections other team members were making.

Darius "Dare" Lyton had chosen the heaviest rifle available, a projectile weapon with oversized exploding rounds. While they hoped not to have to kill any of the enemies they would encounter, since theoretically they were all on the same side, they couldn't depend upon it. The man had selected less lethal options for pistols and grenades, fortunately.

Kyra "Books" Venn had decided to equip herself with support and nonlethal gear. A bandolier across her chest held a dozen knockout gas grenades and the holsters at her hips looked like they held stun pistols. She'd selected an energy rifle, which generally proved less lethal than the alternatives. She also had extra medkits strapped to her belt and each thigh. He hoped that would turn out to be excessive but planned to carry an additional one as well, in case.

Sebastian "Strings" Welker, the team's newest member when Jax had left it, had selected a mostly standard kit: projectile rifle, energy pistol, and a stun baton strapped to his leg. He carried the demo pouch against the possibility they'd need to breach any barriers along the way.

Thomas "Edison" Sparks had stepped in to replace Jax when Wasp took over the squad's leadership. He was short and muscular, with a crazy shock of blonde hair that stuck up as much as the Special Forces' length requirement would permit. The man looked vaguely like his finger had gotten caught in an electrical socket, which doubtless explained his nickname. He chose a shotgun in place of a rifle and crisscrossing bandoliers of different shell options for it. His backpack carried the team's sensor gear, and he had toolkits strapped to his thighs.

Finally, Beatrice "Wasp" O'Leary had selected standard equipment as well. She would coordinate her squad's actions while Jax directed his, and he would follow her lead whenever possible.

Unfortunately, his team was down a couple of people. They'd all agreed that Ethan Kimmel's best role would be to thwart any effort on the other ship's part to use their internal systems against the boarders, should the power come back up. They'd be able to plug in a connector to give him access, so there was no reason for him to abandon the safety of their ship to do it. Trianna and Cia would remain in the *Grace's* pilot compartment, ready to fight if needed or fly in to pick them up if things went wrong. While one of them probably could've handled it, Cia didn't want to trust both the jamming and the piloting to a single person in case either required more attention than expected.

So, that left him, Verrand, Sirenno, and Marshall. The others wore their standard Academy gear. Jax had chosen Special Forces uniform and armor, plus a pair of pistols, a pair of batons, and one of the heavy rifles with the grenade launcher underneath. He was confident they had the fire-power to handle whatever they would face on the other side. An extra med-pack and a variety of other random useful items were in his pouches.

Cia gave them the warning that they were five minutes out from leaving jump, and they all sealed their helmets and headed to the airlock. When they emerged into real space and the panel slid aside, they got their first view of the Intelligence Division ship with their own eyes. They'd reviewed the schematics over and over during the transit and knew what to expect. Still, it seemed bigger than he'd thought it was, easily three or four times the size of the *Grace*.

They'd modified the heavy grapnel gun in the airlock so its cable attached to a hardpoint on the ship, rather than terminating in the weapon. Athena assisted him in aiming, and he squeezed the trigger when she told him to. The heavy magnet flew across to the other ship and adhered to its skin. Then the winch drew the line taut between the two. He reached up, grabbed it, and gave it as hard a yank as he could. It didn't budge. He reported, "We're attached. Try not to move the ship and kill us all." Cia laughed. He gestured at Lyton. "Dare, you're first."

The man gave him a grin. "Off to save the day, that's me." He attached a small, motorized, wheeled device to the cable and snapped a carabiner onto the line as a backup. The machine started moving and pulled him along the line toward the other ship. Each of them followed in turn, with Jax bringing up the rear. They'd considered using propellant packs and flying over, but given that the Academy team didn't have any experience with them, this was a safer, if slower, option.

When he'd detached himself from the line on the enemy ship's hull and activated his mag boots, Athena gave them all a path to the target. They jogged in a double column toward it while holding their rifles ready in case enemies materialized unexpectedly. As they ran past a large anti-ship turret, Jax shook his head. "That right there could ruin our day."

O'Leary laughed. "Oh, I'm sure if the ship had power right now, they'd have all sorts of things competing for the honor of ruining our day."

When they reached the hatch, Sparks reported, "There's atmosphere inside." He knelt beside it. "Everybody stand back." He found the right spot and flipped open a cover to reveal the manual override. He stuck a universal handle into the gear and turned it until the hatch smashed open on its hinges from the force of the air inside escaping. When the flow ran out, they all dropped in and pulled the door closed above them.

Although they could've removed their helmets after the airlock filled with atmosphere, they'd decided to keep them on throughout the mission, both for additional defense against weapons and to address the possibility that the ship might wind up depressurized at some point. Evacuating the vessel's oxygen was their ultimate fallback plan to send the crew into unconsciousness due to lack of air. The dangers involved made it a less than desirable option, especially with the ship's systems down so they couldn't easily restore the others' ability to breathe.

The Special Forces soldiers opened the inner hatch, and the teams flowed out into a room filled with lockers and EVA suits. Jax found a computer port near the airlock controls and slotted in one of the connectors. "You're in, Kimmel." The slot stood out even in the weird view that the night vision function of his helmet provided in the darkened vessel.

He replied, "I see the connection. If the ship gets power, I'll be ready to hack in."

O'Leary said, "Bridge is forward, and we have about half the ship to cover before we get there. We're going to stay together and go right down the middle. My squad is first. Axe's squad, keep an eye on the rear. Odd numbers watch left, evens right. If we get into a fight, you Academy folks should pick your shots carefully. Those of us in front of you would like to avoid any friendly fire incidents."

To only his group, Jax added, "Her squad members are liable to move unpredictably in our view since they have a sense of what the others will do based on training and experience. Although I know you're all good, that doesn't mean you can ignore Wasp's warning. So be extra careful. Of course, if something threatens me, everyone shoot it a lot."

The others laughed. Verrand said, "Well, we wouldn't want to risk losing Athena, right?"

Jax pointed at her. "Exactly. If that's what you need to think to get the job done and save me, I can accept that."

O'Leary ordered, "Let's move out," and they started stalking toward the bridge. His display showed that the ship's passages were laid out more or less in a grid shape, with long corridors on the left, right, and center connected by cross lanes at regular intervals. When they planned the action, he'd at least thought there would be emergency lighting active, but whatever software changes the Academy had made, it had killed everything. *Thank heaven for sensors and night vision. Maybe we'll get lucky, and they won't have either of them.*

Athena snorted. "And maybe there will be a room filled with candy along the way."

Shut it. Also, now I'm hungry. You suck. They only made it as far as the nearest major intersection, less than a minute's travel, before they encountered the first defenders. Their sensors picked them up as thermal images ahead of time, so they knew they were there, but no one expected them to stick guns around the corner and fire without aiming. Fortunately, Special Forces armor was designed to withstand military-grade weapons, and these weren't that powerful. O'Leary said, "Sidearms," in a disgusted voice as if the inconvenience of such a weak attack was an insult. "Books, I bet they're not wearing helmets."

"On it, Boss." The first time he'd heard her referred to that way on the planet, it had been a shock to realize that what he thought of as his call sign belonged to someone else. Now, it was just weird, and he had to force himself not to respond to it. She hurled a grenade into the inter-section where it exploded in a cloud of gas. The firing became uneven, then stopped entirely. A body slumped into the corridor, and O'Leary ordered the teams to advance.

They found four uniformed crew members helmet-less and unconscious. O'Leary ordered, "Einstein, give them a shot so they don't wake up for a while, then catch up. The rest of you keep moving." They encountered another similar ambush a few intersections down, the common crew of the ship doing their best against a far more formidable opponent. Jax respected the effort, although he wished they'd lay down and surrender.

As they moved forward, Sparks announced, "Contact ahead. Electrical."

O'Leary replied, "So, they found some armor, or we're about to meet some robots. Dare, you're in front. Edison, beside him. I have the middle, Strings and Books behind me." Jax gripped his rifle and trained it forward, deeply frustrated by being relegated to the operational second string. He fully understood and agreed with the reasoning behind the move and tried hard not to think of it as a demotion.

He'd figured they wouldn't reach the bridge without encountering a tougher foe, and that belief was confirmed when four grenades banked off the hallway walls, landed among them, and exploded in a cacophony of light and sound.

CHAPTER TWENTY-SIX

They'd been fairly confident going into the missions that the ship's defenders wouldn't have incendiary munitions, or at least wouldn't use them except as a last resort. The likelihood of catastrophic unintended consequences was simply too high. Their suits compensated for the flash-bangs automatically since the immediate detection of danger dimmed their visors and muted their audio pick-ups. Thus, when the squad of enemies appeared in front of them anticipating that they'd be reeling from the initial attack, they were ready for them instead.

What they weren't ready for was the advanced weaponry the defenders carried. The first one raised something that looked like a flamethrower, but it discharged a liquid stream that turned out to be nitrogen, based on its effects. Lyton went down as his frost-covered suit seized up and shorted out under the attack. The other enemy in the front rank carried a weapon with a similar structure, but instead of launching a liquid, it emitted a cone of forked electricity that reached out to envelop

Sparks. For a moment, it seemed as if the absorption built into the armor would be adequate to defeat the incoming damage, but then he started to jerk and twitch, and a scream of pain came over the comm before he fell beside his squadmate.

The team from the Academy made noises of surprise and alarm, while the Special Forces soldiers simply acted. Weapons fire went in the other direction to be absorbed or deflected by their enemies' armor, which was also of a higher quality than they'd anticipated the defenders would have. *Stupid Intelligence Division bastards. Of course they have researchers working on weapons and armor.*

Athena replied, "Less complaining, more shooting."

Jax nodded, grabbed an incendiary grenade, and loaded it into his launcher. It arced over his allies' heads and landed amongst his enemies. It exploded and coated their armor in flaming adhesive gel, and one of the four fell to the floor. The front two fired again, but the element of surprise was no longer on their side.

The electricity reached out toward O'Leary, who threw herself backward to avoid it and only caught a glancing blow as she landed on her back. Her absorption circuits blew with a loud *snap*, and he knew she wouldn't be able to take another one. His grenade must have impacted the freeze gun wielder's aim because his shot went into the ceiling. The third one still standing fired for the first time, and the two Special Forces soldiers in front of him fell to their knees, retching.

Athena said, "Ultra low-frequency sonic weapon, causes nausea. Seems to be conical or short-range, or it would've reached us, too." His helmet squealed as she made an adjustment. "That should compensate. Copying the change to the others."

Good work. He ran forward past the prone Special Forces soldiers while yanking out his baton and a pistol as he let the rifle fall on its strap across his chest. He reached the front two, who were struggling to bring their weapons around to fire at him, and slashed the baton in his left hand to smash down on the freeze gun. It knocked the weapon out of his opponent's grip, and Jax released the baton, turned, lifted the arm of the one with the electrical rifle, and shoved his pistol up into the joint where the limb connected to the defender's torso.

He pulled the trigger, and the round exploded immediately upon leaving the barrel. It separated the man's arm from his body and destroyed the pistol, the gauntlet of Jax's suit, and the skin of the hand that had gripped it. His suit sealed at the wrist, keeping his internal air where it belonged, and he stared down at the metal fingers now showing where what had looked like a human hand had been. The one with the sonic weapon raised it and fired, the smug smile on his face arrogant and dismissive. It transformed into a frown when the shot had no effect. Jax balled his metal hand into a fist, flowed forward, and punched it through the transparent visor of the man's helmet, flattening his nose and knocking him onto his back.

He kicked the weapons aside, slammed the one who had fired the freeze gun into the wall until he dropped to the floor, and headed back to check on his fallen allies. Other team members moved forward to deal with the neutered defenders. Despite several attempts to reboot it, they were unable to get Lyton's armor functioning again. Athena marked a nearby storage compartment, and they carried him in and helped him out of the gear. He was dazed but not visibly injured. Jax said, "Marshall, you're going to stay with him. Anyone comes through that door without clearing it with you first, they go down."

The man looked like he might complain but nodded instead. "Got it."

"Good." They got Sparks moving again, although like O'Leary, his suit's ability to deal with electrical damage was fatally compromised. They headed forward again.

Verrand asked, "Are they able to track us?"

He replied, "They certainly know they've lost contact with the ones we took out. But unless the ship powers up, they shouldn't have access to sensors or anything."

At that moment, as if he'd made it happen by calling attention to it, the ship's lights came back on. Sirenno observed, more calmly than Jax would've expected, "That's probably not good."

Kimmel replied, "I'm on it. Outer layer access already. The codes we have are partially effective, and I should be able to get in soon. In the meantime though, you might want to go faster."

O'Leary remarked, "Can't see a reason to argue with the man. Let's move it. Strings, you're point. Then me, then Books, then the rest. Go." Sparks stepped in line in front of him, and Jax prepared himself to push the soldier out of the way if any electrical attack occurred. *Athena, do you have any access to their systems?*

She replied, "They have a wireless network, and I'm working on it now."

Anything I can do to help?

"Get to the bridge and get this thing shut down before me being in the system is necessary."

He chuckled. *Way to put the responsibility on me. Thanks.*

They ran into another squad of enemies, these fortunately equipped with ordinary weapons. Sirenno went down with a wound to the chest during the exchange of fire, and Sparks took an energy blast that again shorted out his suit and dropped him to the deck. They left that duo behind, as Sirenno was still able to hold a rifle and defend his comrade, and advanced as quickly as they could move.

They heard the buzzing sound and sensed the electrical signal on their scanners before the pair of flying sentries whirred into the hallway. Their first attack was still too fast to counter, and everyone dropped prone as projectiles and energy blasts flew over their heads. They fired back at the devices, which deployed metal shields with small holes for their weapons to fire through, and returned the attack. The projectiles struck them this time, but they weren't designed to defeat the kind of armor Special Forces troops wore. A cry of pain came from behind Jax, but he didn't allow it to distract him. They returned fire and again failed to get through the shields. He was reaching for a grenade when, suddenly, the drones stopped attacking and simply hovered.

Kimmel said, "I don't know how long I can hold them." The members of the teams who were still capable ran forward and physically battered them to the deck with batons and the butts of the rifles. They added an electrical blast to the innards of each to make sure they wouldn't reactivate, then hustled ahead, finding no more defenders separating them from their objective.

They burst onto the bridge, which held only the ship's captain, the pilot, and a very scared-looking, tall, thin, mousy man. Jax smiled. "Hello, Quentin. Good to see you again."

CHAPTER TWENTY-SEVEN

Fortunately, the Intelligence Division ship was equipped with a stellar medical facility, and they were able to take care of all the team's injuries easily. They used a cocktail of drugs Athena recommended to render the crew unconscious after strapping them into their bunks, ensuring that they wouldn't be able to send out any word of warning. Cia confirmed their jamming had proven adequate to block any signals and declared she'd be coming over to the ship momentarily.

Jax connected a channel solely to her and said, "No, you're not. We've been over this."

Cia growled, "No, you shared your opinion on the matter. I never agreed to a single thing."

He shook his head although she couldn't see it. "Look, the *Grace* is our backup plan. It's our *only* backup plan. It's entirely possible that if we need you, the ship will need a pilot while someone else fires weapons. You know that you're better than Trianna at both. I need you there. I need to be able to depend upon that backup plan."

"That's so low, jerkwad."

He replied, "It's true, flygirl. There's nothing I'd like more than to have you by my side while I go into ridiculous levels of danger, but I'm relying on you to rescue me if it all goes wrong."

"If it does, and you die because I wasn't right there to help you, I'm going to bring you back to life and kill you again."

He laughed. "I look forward to it."

Athena replied in his head, "As do I. That would be a very interesting experiment."

He sighed. "Athena likes your plan, for what it's worth."

She grumbled but finally complied. Both ships went into jump, and Jax joined the others in the ship's galley, which was about twice the size of the one on the *Grace*. "So, what did everyone find?"

Lyton announced, "We've got some handy-dandy tools for this mission." He tossed a set of small pins on the rectangular metal table that most of them were seated around. The room reminded him of a high school cafeteria more than anything else. "They're transponders, Intelligence Division transponders. If we deactivate ours and activate these, we should read as crew members on the base."

Jax nodded. "Be sure to sock one of those away somewhere for Athena to examine after this is all over. They should allow us to use their weapons, too, which would be useful going forward."

O'Leary asked, "You think there's more to do once we take down this bastard?"

"I do. There's bound to be some other scumbags in his

division who have been enabling him who will step up. Maybe we'll be lucky enough to get most or all of them on this mission, but I'm not ready to count on it. So, let's turn this into an intelligence operation as well as a 'beat the hell out of Zavian Arlox' operation."

The others pounded on the table softly in agreement. Verrand asked, "So, what's our plan, then?"

Jax looked at O'Leary, who nodded for him to continue. "Wasp and I have been talking it over, and there's no way we can boil out of the ship and shoot everything in sight. We'll get our asses handed to us if we try to do that. So, I'm going to have to go in alone first and find a way to make it possible for you all to get out."

His team shook their heads doubtfully, and Marshall asked, "Really? Again?"

Jax laughed. "I get it, really, I do. But in this case, one person will look a lot less suspicious than a bunch of people. And I'm the one with the extra advantage." He tapped his temple to indicate Athena. "I'm afraid I'm the logical choice. I mean, my long history of infiltration ops would've made me the choice anyway, but I have the best chance of success among the people in this group."

There were grumbles, but no one could argue. O'Leary said, "So, we'll get him all kitted up and looking like an intelligence division scumbag, then wait for things to kick off. When they do, we charge out and shoot our way through anyone between us and our target."

Kimmel said, "Between Athena and I, we ought to be able to hack into their systems without a problem. That will at least give us the layout of the place, and ideally we can penetrate deep enough to get control of everything.

The codes on the ship are more recent than the ones we had, although similar enough that we were able to crack them. We'll use them as a starting point for the base and hopefully achieve a similar result."

Athena, visible on one of the monitors, nodded her assent. "I recommend that we lock down the hangar first thing, so no one can use the ships inside to escape. If we accomplish that, there will be no need for any of you to stay with the ship. I can remotely run the sensors and weapons on this vessel no matter where I am and deny anyone who tries to get through."

Jax nodded. "I'm in full agreement with this plan. One more serious word. I'd like us to do our best to avoid loss of life. I know that won't be completely possible, but although these folks are currently our enemies, it's only because their leader has guided them in the wrong direction. He needs to go down, but for everyone else, if wounding will take them out, then wound them. Don't risk yourselves to do it, of course." As many times as he said that to others, he tended not to follow that advice. Hopefully he, too, could avoid killing people unnecessarily. He finished, "Any questions?"

Venn raised her hand, and O'Leary chuckled. "Knock that junk off, Books. What?"

She grinned. "When this is all over, can we keep the ship? I think this would be a pretty nice ride."

Everyone laughed, and O'Leary scowled at her subordinate. "I'll tell you what, Axe, this one here has only gotten worse since you left."

He shrugged. "It takes a special talent to keep the really smart ones in line. You probably don't have the aptitude, but it's okay. I'm sure you'll be a fine captain anyway, once you're done acting."

More laughter rang out, and they broke up to get to work. The ship held all the navigational data needed to arrive at the system with the hidden base exactly as expected. Athena had pulled all the security recordings and used them to create avatar versions of the ship's pilot and captain, and she impersonated them to negotiate their way in.

As they neared the facility, the scale of it became evident. It had seemed like an average size installation in the images, but it was probably half again that big. As the blast doors that secured the hangar slid open ahead of them, it was apparent that four ships the size of the one they were on would fit inside it. Already present were vessels that the computers identified as Confederacy, Snellar, and Krastow, the latter two aliens who weren't aligned with the Coalition. He muttered, "So, more than one alien species is involved and sneaking around behind the Coalition's back."

Athena replied, "It appears Arlox has been up to even more nefarious work than we thought. I mean, one alien race, evil enough. But two? That's piling on."

Jax shook his head. *That really wasn't funny. You clearly don't have an aptitude for humor and should probably quit trying.*

She chuckled. "I found from watching humans that the key to humor is trying everything out and seeing what sticks. Often, the dumbest options are the ones that receive the most laughs. All of *your* jokes, for instance, fall into the categories of either 'stupid' or 'unfunny.'"

No crew was present in the hangar. When they arrived, only one person was visible, up in a large transparent window on the tall space's topmost level. Athena told the flight master that Quentin required a few more minutes to get ready and that an escort should be available outside the hangar for him. The ship's crew would take him that far. Although it was likely an unexpected request, it met with no argument.

The ship's schematics had revealed that the best option for Jax to exit the ship without being seen was through a bottom hatch, right near the landing gear. The huge strut would block sightlines from either side, and he could then do his best to step out and look like he belonged in the hangar. He dropped the few feet to the deck and crouched quietly to ensure no one had spotted him. The place looked new, still kind of shiny and unspoiled. He wondered idly how many places like this Arlox had created and how he'd paid for them all.

Athena noted, "I've added finding that out to our to-do list."

He nodded. *I don't just want him. I want to take down his whole enterprise. I bet Maarsen would agree.* He wore his display glasses since they wouldn't look out of place in a facility like this and followed the path she laid out on it. The uniform fit him well and was standard Intelligence Division issue, dark blue with maroon trim and black logos. He strode through the hangar as if he belonged and exited through a side door rather than the main portal that Arlox's assistant would supposedly be taking. He made an immediate left and headed for the nearest security station.

Getting into the system far enough to get the layout had

been easy. However, Athena was still having challenges getting to the deeper layer where security cameras and networks lay, as was Kimmel. *Any time now, Athena.*

She growled, "My first priority is making sure you can open the door with your biometrics or that I can override it. Getting you cameras is secondary."

Easy for you to say. You're not the one potentially walking into an ambush.

"I kind of am. Now quit whining. You're annoying me."

When he arrived at the security station, the door opened at his touch and revealed two technicians inside wearing uniforms identical to his. They both carried sidearms, as he did, and at the sight of him one turned toward him and went for his weapon, and the other reached for the control panel in front of him. Jax drew his stun pistol, an Intelligence Division version that was functional only because of the transponder attached to his borrowed outfit, and shot the one who was presumably reaching for an alarm.

He stepped forward and slapped the other one's pistol out of line, then snapped the edge of his skin-covered hand into his throat as a distraction. A stun blast took him down as well, and Jax crossed to the control panel and slotted in a connector so Kimmel could have more direct access to the systems.

He returned to stand near the door. "Ethan, Athena, do your thing."

It took about forty-five seconds, but then alarms started to go off throughout the facility. Kimmel reported, "I've created fake fires in several locations and a radiation alarm in the reactor area. The hangar doors are locked down, both the ones to get into the space and the large blast doors. I don't have access to the security systems, however."

Athena added, "I have cameras and sensors and have located Arlox." A map of the station popped into his display glasses, with a yellow line displaying the fastest route to their quarry. Jax snagged the fallen weapons and stuck them in the back of his belt, then re-holstered his. He couldn't restrain a grin. "All right, everyone. Get a move on. We have a date with a very special scumbag, and we don't want to be late."

CHAPTER TWENTY-EIGHT

Jax caught up to his allies as they emerged from the hangar. O'Leary's team quickly dropped the guards who waited there with stun blasts. As he climbed into his heavy armor, Athena displayed station cameras showing the station's fast response. Several security teams were suiting up in heavy armor to deal with the crisis. He called, "Kimmel, can you lock all the doors in the facility?"

The computer expert replied, "Sure. Why?"

"Do it. Any delay we can put in these people's path is a good thing, and we'll route past the locked doors or have you open them when we reach them." He conferred with O'Leary on a private channel, and they agreed it would be best for them to remain as a single group and replicate their tactics from the assault on the Intelligence Division ship. They lined up with the Special Forces troops in front and headed along Athena's indicated path. Unlike the vessel, which had provided a straight line to the target and only a few ways to flank them, the Intelligence base's layout seemed comparatively haphazard, almost maze-like. *I wouldn't put it past Arlox to do that deliberately.*

Athena replied, "It wouldn't be the worst strategy. Sowing confusion everywhere one can."

Shouts of contact rang out from ahead, and Jax threw himself to the side as weapons fire came down the center of the hallway. From the sound of it, the defenders were using heavier weapons than they'd faced on the ship, which made sense. Although the risk of decompression was still present here, one would assume the walls were much thicker than the vessel's hull, and they were deep into the interior of the facility in any case. O'Leary ordered, "Fall back," and they complied, funneling out of the main corridor into side hallways to avoid the projectiles and energy cascading down it.

Jax inquired, "Kimmel, anything you can do with the internal systems to make their lives more difficult?"

"No. Also, now there are people in the system working against me. I can't guarantee I can even keep the current level of lockdown that I have going."

Athena, you have the hangar under control?

"Unless they kill the wireless network, which they likely won't based on their people's needs for surveillance access, absolutely."

Good. "Gotta keep moving, Wasp."

O'Leary growled, "Tell me something I don't know. Let's go with grenades." The sound of launchers firing and canisters rolling echoed down the hallway, and a mix of knockout gas and incendiaries went off.

Sparks reported, "They're all still up. Electrical and thermal both."

He could envision O'Leary's frown from the tone of her voice. "Well, of course they'd have heavy armor. Why wouldn't they? So this will be more of a fair fight than the last one. I hate fair fights."

Jax laughed to himself, having said the same thing on any number of occasions. He suggested, "Some of us could circle, try to hit them from the sides."

She replied, "Except they might see you coming like they saw us. Still, I don't have a better idea. Books, Strings, hook around from the left. Jax, take one of yours and go right. Everyone else, let's give them some more grenades to keep them occupied."

Transponder signals appeared on his map as colored dots that showed his allies in green and their enemies in red overlaid on a wireframe schematic of the facility. He tapped Marshall on the shoulder and led the other man to a nearby hallway, then pushed him aside and dove to the ground as a turret suddenly dropped out of the ceiling and spat rounds at them. He blasted it apart with a sustained burst of projectiles from his rifle and growled, "Kimmel, what the hell?"

Their computer expert sounded frazzled. "There's more of them than of me. I'm working as fast as I can, but there will be gaps here and there."

Athena, can you help him?

"I already am. However, I'm also facing pushback against my access to the cameras and other surveillance systems. We wouldn't want to lose track of Arlox's whereabouts."

Good point. What's the bastard doing?

"Hiding in the lab where he was when all this started."

Hooray for overconfidence. I guess he thinks we won't reach him. I can't wait to smash that arrogance out of him. The hard part will be choosing whether to use my rifle or my baton. While Jax conferred with the AI, he led Marshall forward until they reached the corner of the hallway where the enemy troops were.

She replied, "Why not both?"

He laughed. *I like the way you think.* "Marshall, we go when the next attack hits. You take the left one, and I'll take the right. Remember that thing I said about not trying to kill anyone? They're in heavy armor, so we don't get that option. They need to go down before they take us down."

"Affirmative." There was no fear in the other man's voice, only determination.

"Wasp, we're ready. Give us a distraction."

"Incoming."

When the grenades went off, Jax ordered, "Go," stepped into the hallway and lifted his rifle. Athena gave him a target, and he sighted in on his enemy's transparent faceplate. The defender was in profile with his back against the wall as he ducked back from the grenades. Jax squeezed the trigger, and heavy projectiles flew out at the soldier. His armor withstood the initial ones, but then he made the mistake of turning toward Jax rather than turning away. It was a natural response, but it allowed the bullets to stitch across the already weakened faceplate. He fell in a spray of red as the armor failed.

Marshall had gone for his opponent's legs, doubtless because a headshot would be too uncertain and the chest plates were always the most well-armored spot. Again, the armor worked as it was supposed to for a few moments, but the weapons his team carried were designed to deal with their level of protection. The man went down. Jax slotted a grenade into his launcher and propelled it into the intersection, where two soldiers stood firing forward down the hallway.

The attack from the side distracted the defenders enough that O'Leary's charge took them down, and in moments, Venn and Welker had dropped their foes as well. Their transponders allowed them to remove the helmets of the ones still alive, and Sparks injected them to ensure they wouldn't wake up until the battle for the facility was over. O'Leary growled, "Forward, people. That took too long."

They encountered an identical group a short while later and used the same tactics to defeat them, but again lost precious time their enemies could use to mobilize a stronger response. Jax shook his head and connected directly to O'Leary. "Wasp, this isn't working. They have more people and firepower than we anticipated."

"Stop telling me things I already know."

He barked a laugh. "Just like old times, eh?"

O'Leary snorted. "Time to split up?"

He nodded. "Yeah. You maintain contact with them and fight a delaying action. Athena can do her best to ghost us in the cameras, and we'll circle and go after Arlox."

"You know this doesn't have a huge chance of success, right?"

"Yeah. I get the tactical disadvantage. The chance of us maintaining secrecy for long is pretty small. But if they come after us, you can go after the bastard. If they come after you, we can go after the bastard. Either way, as long as someone gets him, it's a win."

"And if they come after both of us?

He shrugged. "At least Cia is out there to take word of our failure back to Maarsen and Stephenson. The fight will continue, I'm sure, but no longer with our involvement."

She gave the dark laugh that was typical of Special Forces missions, the one that acknowledged courting death was a dangerous game. "Let's do our best to avoid that outcome."

"You got it. Good luck."

"You too."

He activated the channel for his team. "Athena, make sure that Kimmel has access to cameras and sensors as well. Ethan, you need to assist the Special Forces squad in navigating to their destination. Athena will guide our group."

He offered a clipped reply. "Acknowledged."

"Athena, we want to stay unnoticed for as long as we can. Take us along whatever route works for that."

"On it." She led them through a twisting and turning route that avoided many of the red dots on the map. The problem was that they were spreading out, either by design or at random, which reduced the advantage of his team's access to the cameras and their transponders. Eventually, contact was inevitable. He was forced to stop at a T-intersection with another corridor. They needed to head to the left, but two red dots moved toward them from that direction. He asked, "Visual?"

The camera view popped into his display and showed a pair of heavily armored defenders marching down the hallway. Their gear was equal to his and superior to his team's. He growled inwardly, wishing he'd had the foresight to make them all wear heavy armor despite the fact that it would have been counterproductive. Using such equipment required extensive training, and without it, they would bumble around like characters in an old slapstick film.

"Okay. Everyone but me tosses grenades. You'll bounce them off the wall so you don't have to expose yourselves. Then I'll go out and take them down. You do *not* want them shooting at you. Those rifles will tear holes through your armor, then through you."

The others nodded. Sirenno remarked, "Good plan. I like this plan. Unrelatedly, do you think Kimmel needs anyone to help him back at the ship?"

They laughed, and Jax said a small word of thanks to the universe for providing him with such strong-willed allies. He paused a moment, waiting until the angles were right, then ordered, "Throw."

CHAPTER TWENTY-NINE

As the grenades detonated, Jax charged around the corner. The Intelligence Division troops were well-trained and confident that their armor would protect them from the incoming damage. The rifles were already coming up toward him, and his eyes widened in surprise as he saw that they looked even heavier than his. His finger tightened on the trigger automatically, but the bullets sparked off their suits without penetrating.

He growled, "What the hell," as he dropped into a slide. His armor scraped along the facility's plastic floor, which slowed his momentum faster than he expected. His hope had been to at least knock the legs out from underneath at least one of them since a problem with heavy armor was that if you didn't use it on a very regular basis, getting upright when you fell was a decided challenge.

The move caused the bullets to fly over his head. He planted his feet, used his momentum to lift him back up to a crouch, then drove ahead to hammer the one on the right-hand side with his shoulder. The man dipped his rifle's stock to block, but the impact was powerful enough to send him flying anyway. The collision stopped Jax's forward motion, and he whipped a backfist at the opponent on his left while twisting his torso and putting all the power of his prosthetic limb into the blow. It clanged off the armored figure's helmet, and she turned to face him with a smile.

He breathed, "Damn bloody researchers." He leapt to his right as she pulled the trigger, and the bullets deflected from his chest armor.

Athena reported, "If those had been head-on rather than at an angle, they would've penetrated."

"Of course they would have," he cursed. On his right, the other one was struggling to regain his feet. Jax dashed to him and yanked at his arm while twisting his own body in such a way that the other man lost his balance and stumbled. Jax propelled him toward the woman, then lifted his rifle and aimed it. Right before he pulled the trigger, he saw the damage her shots had inflicted and realized it was too dangerous to use.

He hit the quick release on the weapon's strap and threw the gun at the two figures. She'd reflexively fired a couple of rounds at her partner as he careened toward her, but now they were both up and facing Jax. He charged the duo, slammed into them, and knocked them both into the wall. He grabbed the woman's weapon and ripped at it, and her strap broke. He hurled the rifle down the hall.

Going for his sidearms wasn't a valid option since unless he breached their armor, the weapons wouldn't be strong enough to have an effect. He thought, *Here goes nothing*, and formed a spearpoint with the fingers of his right hand, pushing the digits against each other to create as small an area of impact as possible. He stepped forward, twisted his hips, and drove it at the woman's faceplate.

Although almost everyone used transparent panels for the front of their helmets, in case they lost internal displays, the practice came with a trade-off. The material was inherently weaker than other armor plate options. The cold rush of adrenaline had filled him at the start of the move, Athena's contribution to the attack, and his pointed fingers pierced the faceplate, cracked it, and caused a piece to fall away. He re-chambered the arm and punched a fist into the gap he'd created, widening it enough that the barrel of the stun pistol he lifted in his left hand could fit.

He pulled the trigger and enough electricity transferred to the woman that her eyebrows stood on end before she fell. The man behind her fired, and Jax felt the rounds penetrate his suit and deflect from his left arm as he twisted out of the way. One slammed off his helmet and made his ears ring, but he dove forward into a roll and grabbed the sharp-edged fragment that had fallen from the woman's faceplate in his metal hand.

He popped up and jammed it directly at the man's eyes. His foe backpedaled, reflexively afraid of the sharp and pointy thing being thrust at his face, and Jax used the distance to deliver a kick that sent his foe sprawling. He ran toward the man and leapt into the air before he could recover, landing with his armored knees on his foe's chest plate. It crumpled, and the man lifted his arms in surrender as Jax rose to pummel him again. Jax motioned at his helmet, and the other man removed it. Verrand pressed a syringe against the side of his neck and pushed the plunger. Jax gave her a quizzical look, and she shrugged. "Borrowed some from Sparks."

He nodded. "Good work." *Athena, am I compromised?*

The AI snorted. "Only mentally. But your suit probably won't take too many more direct shots in the chest before it lets one through. Also, more blows to your left arm could render it unusable. The metal is tough, but not indestructible."

Add convincing Juno to create indestructible arms for me to our to-do list, please.

"Noted."

He checked his display, which indicated they needed to move out. Another pair of red dots headed in their direction from behind. "Come on people, let's hustle."

He kept an eye on the green dots that represented the Special Forces team, gratified to see that they stayed more or less in motion, although more attention was being paid to them by the red dots than to his team. *Good work keeping them off us, Athena.*

"I've created images of you in the system all over the base. They haven't yet figured out that they're duplicates and are sending teams to check them out. It won't last."

Kimmel blurted, "Damn, I lost connection to the security overrides. Be careful. I'll get them back," he promised.

What does that mean for us, Athena?

"Nothing at the moment. Keep moving."

Jax complied and grew increasingly hopeful as they neared the yellow-outlined lab that was their primary objective. *Arlox still inside?*

"Yes. Him, some other people, and some aliens."

Fighters?

"Doesn't look like it. More like politicians."

He grinned. *Excellent.* When they rounded the next corner, an intense wash of fire flowed over his helmet. He shouted a warning and ducked back into the previous corridor. "What the hell was that?"

Athena replied, "Security robot. Doesn't have a transponder, and the security cameras are apparently programmed not to notice them."

"Any suggestions?"

"Retreat is out of the question, so I guess you have to fight it."

Jax sighed. "I was afraid you were going to say that." He turned to Sirenno. "Give me your rifle." The other man complied. "I'll go out and grab its attention. You all do what you can and try your best not to hit me. I should be able to take a few shots, but eventually you'll chew through even my armor." They nodded. "Okay, here we go."

He charged around the corner, this time prepared for the wash of fire that came at him. His suit was adequate to it, and Athena switched his display to electrical and fine-tuned it so he could see his opponent's shape through the flames. It was a tall cylinder with four arms, each of which ended in a fork. The upper tine contained the barrel of a weapon, and the lower one a wicked-looking spike. It had four legs. He'd seen similar setups before and knew it would probably scuttle like a spider. Fighting spikes appeared to have been added to the bottom appendages as well.

In place of a head, it had a series of gun barrels arrayed in a circle. It was an amalgam of two designs he'd seen before. The bottom half minus the spikes was for street patrols in occupied areas, and the four arms and rotating skull were from a frontline combat droid model rendered obsolete by heavier armor. However, he imagined the Intelligence Division researchers had found a way around that problem.

The barrels on top spun and spat projectiles at him. Jax raised his arms in front of him to shield his face and felt himself slow from the sheer force of the impacts. *Jolt me, Athena. Everything you've got.* He spent the additional energy in a burst of speed that delivered him to the robot, then lifted his rifle and stuck it where the join between the top weapon and the cylinder should have been.

It turned out to be seamless, not even enough of a gap for him to get the rifle barrel into it. The torso cylinder spun and one of the arms whipped around to strike him, throwing him into the corridor wall. A leg snapped up, and he blocked it with a downward punch. Electricity coursed over his suit as the thing used another arm to attack him, and a small gauge in his display showed how long he had until his absorption ran out.

Fortunately, it wasn't all that much more powerful than a standard stun weapon. The thing's algorithm probably suggested it would be the most effective choice if his suit was compromised, and thus worth testing. *Oops. Stupid robot is stupid.* He shuffled close to its torso while using his armored shins to block the strikes from its legs and staying under the barrels that whirred over his head. Its torso spun, and he moved around with it by grabbing the arms to keep himself in place. When he faced back toward his team, he planted his feet and yelled, "Now."

Weapons appeared around the corner at three heights

and fired a stream of energy at the robot. Simultaneously, he chopped the edge of his right hand in at the spot where the arm connected to the cylinder. It gave slightly, and he pounded it several more times until it finally broke off. He stabbed his hand directly forward into the stump and knocked it back into the robot, which created a hole. He lost control of the other arm during the process, and shouted in pain as a spike pierced the armor on his left shoulder from behind and came out the front, pinning him to his metallic opponent.

Jax knew its next action would be to tear him off and toss him away so it could shoot him with the spinning barrels on its head. He went with the only option he could think of. He grabbed one of his grenade launcher's incendiary rounds from the bandolier across his chest, jammed it into the hole as far as he could, then punched it. The detonation hurled him backward, but it also damaged the robot, which fell over. He heard the muffled sounds of his team shouting instructions to shoot into it while it was down, followed by the sizzle of their weapons. The power to his armor had failed, and he couldn't move. Sirenno was the first to enter his field of vision. "Jax, you okay?"

He got his wits about him again and nodded inside his helmet. *Athena, can you get me restarted?"*

"Negative. The explosion damaged the suit's internal power relays. We would need more tools and time than we have here."

Could Sparks do it? He remembered the toolkits the man carried.

"Maybe, but not in a timely fashion. Plus, they're a little busy right now."

As much as he hated the idea, he ordered, "Okay, then pop it."

Every heavy armor suit had a small set of self-powered actuators on it that permitted escape in a situation like this. The pieces of his armor detached from one another, and his team pulled them away. When he climbed out, Verrand snapped, "You're bleeding. Hold still for a minute." A self-adhesive bandage clawed into the skin of his back, then she came around to his chest and applied one to the exit wound as well.

He growled, "Ow."

She slapped him on the unwounded side of his chest. "Don't be a baby."

He shook his head. "Athena. Tell me there's not another one of those nearby."

"I can't confirm it. The good news is that Kimmel's back in the system and should hopefully be able to shut them down or draw them away."

"Okay. Then let's get a move on. We can't let these bastards slow us down any more." He went to retrieve his rifle, only to discover that it had been destroyed. He drew his energy pistol instead. "Nothing's going to stop us from making sure this is Arlox's worst day ever."

CHAPTER THIRTY

They encountered no additional resistance until they reached the laboratory door. They'd known the defenders would have sentries guarding the space, and Jax counted himself lucky when they weren't in the heaviest suits. *They thought they could stop us before we got here.*

Athena replied, "Foolish people."

He laughed. *Damn right.* He turned to his team. "Okay, those jerks need to go down. Here's what we're going to do."

Two minutes later, Marshall and Verrand jumped around the corner into view of the guard pair and covered them with bullets. They staggered back under the unexpected onslaught, and Jax ran forward to deliver a double punch directly into their faceplates. His prosthetic fists penetrated while smashing the duo against the wall and dropping them. A blast door descended from the ceiling.

Athena growled, "The guards must have had a failsafe. I can't keep it open." He palmed the normal door, which she'd unlocked, and dove through in a roll. He tumbled up to his feet to find the politicians cringing and Arlox holding up his hands.

The Intelligence Director said, "Jackson, thank you for coming." The sound of the bulkhead slamming shut informed him he was on his own. Arlox smiled at the others. "See? As I promised. All copies of the AI, right here for our use."

Athena?

She replied, "Kimmel has locked down the automatic defenses in the room. Stun turrets are positioned in several locations, and more heavily powered projectile ones in others. He's giving his full attention to keeping them deactivated."

Tell the other teams to join together for defense. However Wasp thinks best. He crossed his arms and shook his head at Arlox. "Oh, please. As if this is some grand scheme of yours."

The man gave a soft smile. "Who's to say it isn't? In any case, we couldn't have hoped for a better outcome."

"My people will have full control of your facility in no time. You're done, Zavian." He put a little sneer into the man's name.

His enemy replied, "I don't think so. See, when you thought you were all the way into our systems, you didn't realize there are places that even we don't want to watch over." Doors slid up at the sides of the room to reveal two alien guards on his right, one from each species, and two on his left. They boiled inward as the former pair pulled edged weapons and the latter fired pistols. Jax dove to avoid the initial barrage and slid behind a large exam chair that looked a lot like the one he'd been in when Marshall had added Athena to his brain. *Suggestions?*

"Beat the hell out of them."

Okay then, let's do that thing. He popped up and ran toward Arlox, knowing the guards would move to protect the man. When they shifted their balance, he stopped, spun, drew his pistols, and fired them at the two humans. One struck its target, and the stun charge dropped the man. The energy blast missed as the other guard dodged. He turned to face the aliens, both of whom were tall, strong-looking and approached at an angle to him. There was no time to shoot them before they forced him to defend himself.

They swung together, and he spun away to close the distance to the one on his right. He hammered a backfist into that one's skull and kicked at the other. Jax almost lost his foot as a blade swept across in a block but dropped to the floor so it passed over his leg. He rolled, narrowly avoided a stomp from the one he'd punched, then rolled back as that guard stabbed down with his sword. Jax released his pistols and grabbed the blade in his left hand before it could pierce him, then chopped his right across to snap it in the middle. *Kind of nice not having to worry about cutting myself, anyway.*

"Roll," Athena ordered, and he complied without hesitation. The other alien's sword missed his head by an inch, and he kept the roll going until he could get to his feet. A laser blast burned into the formerly unwounded side of his chest. He gasped and dropped to one knee, then threw himself to the floor to avoid the follow-up shot.

He realized he was still holding the broken blade and

breathed, "Athena, help me," as he rose again and whipped his arm forward like he was hurling a javelin. She took over to adjust his aim and increase his power, and the shard of the alien weapon flew across the room and stabbed the other human guard deep in the chest. He noticed in passing that the politicians were cowering and Arlox was moving, but there was no time to react to them.

He rose warily to his feet and faced the aliens. The one holding the sword was advancing, and the other had drawn a pair of small daggers. He twitched toward the human he'd taken down, but the one wielding the longer blade moved into his path. "Okay, let's do this." He charged in a circle away from that opponent and toward the one with the knives. The alien guard seemed happy to meet him and waded in with a flurry of slashes and stabs. Jax took them all on his prosthetic arms. Sparks shot out at the impact, but none damaged him.

He was suddenly inside the alien's guard. He crouched slightly, twisted his body, and exploded upward to ram his palm into the underside of the being's chin. It lifted the creature off its feet and snapped its neck with a loud crack. Jax's left arm shot out to grab one of the daggers as it fell. He tossed it in the air while thinking back to his juggling lessons, then whipped his right hand forward as he caught it by the point and threw it in a single blurred motion. He had no idea whether the action was him, Athena, or the two of them in perfect harmony.

The alien's block wasn't fast enough, and the blade sank deep into its forehead. It fell backward, and Jax searched for more foes. His last sight of Arlox showed him sitting in a large chair in a hidden closet as a transparent canopy lowered over it. The man gave him an arrogant smile as the escape pod blasted off from the base. Belatedly, he realized the other man had been holding a metal case, likely with whatever copies existed of Athena. He shouted, "Oh, *hell* no." *Athena, get me Cia.* He scooped up his pistols and kept them trained on the remaining people in the room.

The pilot's voice broke into the comm channel. "Jax, are you okay? Athena has been keeping us updated, more or less."

He choked out a laugh and peered down at the scorched burn hole in his chest and the blood soaking the bandage on the other side. "I've been better. More importantly, Arlox just shot out of here. You have him?"

She growled, "Nothing on the sensors. Let me try the different bands." After a few seconds, she reported, "Still nothing."

Athena replied, "He probably has sensor countermeasures built-in. A lot of interesting research has been going on here. Start pinging the nanoparticles and don't stop."

Cia replied, "On it."

He coughed. "Do you think that will work?"

Athena replied, "It depends on the delay. It should at least give a general sense of where he is."

Cia cut in, "I have him now. He's going really fast toward a jump point. Is that thing capable?"

Jax nodded. "It's probably based on the lover's coffin. Those can go through jump. You need to stop him, Cia." *Athena, can you get me a view of what she's seeing?*

"Working on it."

The pilot grumbled, "Damn, that thing is fast. It'll take

us a few minutes to catch up. Do you think it has weapons?"

He replied, "I'm not sure I'd put anything past him at this point. Maybe you should blast it with your missile."

"I already have it primed and locked. We can use it as a last resort, but I think we have a better option."

Jax smiled when he remembered their first flights together. "The EMP?"

"Yep. The *Grace* has enough boom to take out a full-size ship. It should be able to deal with that little thing, even if it's hardened."

"If it can't, there's always the missile."

"Yep." Shouting came from her copilot in the background, and Cia yelped.

Jax demanded, "What's going on?"

"It's armed. Lasers, surprisingly high-power. He's burned off part of a wing."

"Shoot him down. Don't wait."

He could hear the scowl in Cia's voice. "Oh, no bloody way. I need to have some words with this bastard."

He cautioned, "Cia. This is really important. He can't get away."

"I get it, Jax. Trust me. I've got this."

His first instinct was to argue, but he pushed it away. His second instinct was to offer advice that she didn't need, but he shunted that aside too. "I trust you. Completely. Go kick his ass."

He dug for his display glasses to watch the view from the *Grace*'s nose camera as it wove through the laser blasts seeking it, which seemed to grow increasingly frantic as the gap between them diminished. When she was close enough, Cia advised, "Talk to you on the other side." The running lights on her ship suddenly went dark. He fretted during the seeming eternity while he waited for the *Grace*'s systems to come back up. Both ships were still heading on their original trajectories, so there was no way to tell whether the EMP had disabled the pod. The only positive sign was that the laser blasts had ceased. Now, it was more or less a race to see who could get their vessel back up first.

The *Grace* won. Athena gave him a rear view as the cargo hatch opened and a vacuum-suited figure fired a grapnel gun to latch on to the pod. Its motor kicked into gear and reeled the small ship in. Cia crowed, "We've got him. We'll cut him out of there, sedate him, and come give you a hand."

Jax grinned and slumped to the floor while keeping the stun pistol pointed at the trio of other figures in the room. *Athena, see what you can do about getting the door open. I don't think I'm going to be able to stay conscious much longer.*

She snorted. "Always leaving the hard work for me. That's just like you, Jax."

He decided that diplomacy was for the birds and shot the politicians with the stun gun shortly before he succumbed to the encroaching darkness.

CHAPTER THIRTY-ONE

The Academy's "back yard" was done up in lights and decorations that outshone the other parties he'd attended there. Professor Maarsen walked around the place with a huge smile on his face, and Jax couldn't help grinning at the sight. The evidence they'd found at the base, plus Zavian Arlox's capture, had given the older man closure on something that had vexed him for ages.

Jax's team was present, as was Wasp's team, as he'd come to think of them. He'd been impressed with the way they worked together and only a little put out that the transition away from his leadership seemed to have been handled so adroitly. He was sure he'd get over it, eventually.

Athena quipped, "Please, with your ego? It'll take forever for you to get past that one."

He shook his head. *Shut it.* Something had happened during the last weeks, a bonding of sorts that made it impossible for him to keep the AI out of his thoughts but also made it natural for her to be there. He considered it a feature rather than a bug, generally, although she still had to work on her understanding of when to speak and when to be quiet.

"Do not."

Proves my point. He grinned wider as Major Stephenson approached him and held out a hand. Jax shook it, and the woman pulled him into an unexpected hug. When she let him go, she commented, "So. You did it. Nicely done."

"We did it. This was a serious team effort. Well, a serious *teams* effort if you get right down to it. What do you hear?"

She shrugged. "They're cleaning house in Intelligence and bringing in someone from outside to run it. They found evidence that his philosophy had spread throughout the organization. A lot of people are getting reassigned."

"And the others involved in his game? The aliens and the Confederacy?"

"We informed their governments, of course, but that's about all we could do." She looked at him suspiciously. "What's interesting is that Arlox kept talking about a case that he had with him in the pod, but it appears to have vanished."

He nodded. "I saw it in his lap when he blasted off. Never saw it again." That was true, although he'd had to choose his words with care for it to be so. Cia had destroyed it at Athena's direction before the ship had joined them at the base.

Her expression didn't change. "Uh-huh. Sure."

Jax laughed. "Really. Captain's honor."

"Which brings us to the reason I'm here." She gestured

around at the festivities. "I'm not all that fond of parties like this. I prefer a noisy tavern and bitter drafts."

He'd been expecting something like this for a while and appreciated that she'd come to tell him in person. He'd gone pretty far afield, especially where the box he hadn't seen was concerned, and figured that he'd ticked off some higher-ups. *Well, at least I have a pretty good backup gig, right?*

Athena snorted. "You're happy because you don't have to make a choice. You're a coward."

Correction. We're a coward. His superior officer continued, "I'm getting kicked upstairs. Going to a bigger command. They need someone to replace me, and I told them I'd talk to you about it."

He blinked in surprise. "What?"

She laughed. "They're offering you a promotion. Major Jackson Reese. Has a ring to it. You'd get to stay on the *Cronus* and oversee the three teams. I'd be in charge of your ship and a couple of others."

It took a few seconds before he could speak again, but he eventually found the words. "No. Hell, no. Like, so much no."

Stephenson laughed again. "I figured. The allure of the Academy." She sighed. "It's fine. Lorenzo will step up. She's ready for the job. I was never convinced about you, really." Her smile revealed the lie. "Keep in touch, Jax."

"You know it, Major."

She snorted. "It's Lieutenant Colonel now, thanks, but it's probably time you started calling me Anika."

"All right. Later, Anika."

He turned away so she wouldn't see his sadness at the change. Given his choice, he'd want to have it all. Working with his Special Forces team, working with his Academy team. Roaming the universe, staying at the castle. *But I guess we can't have everything.*

Athena replied, "No, but you might be able to have the most important things. On your eleven."

He looked up and over in the direction she indicated and spotted Juno walking toward him. Her face lit up as she drew near, and he was sure that he wore a stupid smile. They hadn't had much time together since his return, and all of it had been as doctor and patient. He asked, "So, have you figured out those indestructible arms yet?"

She rolled her eyes. "You get state-of-the-art prosthetic technology, and all you do is complain. Honestly."

He laughed and captured one of her hands with his. "Well, I wouldn't want you to get too comfortable resting on your laurels. I mean, I'm pretty awesome as-is, but I'm sure that you can find a way to make me better."

Juno snorted. "I think a lobotomy might help."

Athena observed, "You know, if done right, they could maybe wipe out your personality and leave me in charge. That would work."

Jax shook his head. "My brain friend is on the zombie kick again."

Juno replied, "I know, she asked me about it yesterday."

"When?"

Athena sounded smug. "When you were sleeping. With access to your comm, I can accomplish all sorts of things during your stupid rest periods."

Jax raised a hand. "Never mind. So, I have news."

"You're being promoted."

He threw up his hands. "Why is it everyone knows about everything, and I don't?"

She laughed. "I was watching when you talked to Stephenson. I saw your face. It doesn't take a genius, although I am one."

He lifted an eyebrow. "So, genius, what did I say?"

"You said you're staying at the Academy, based on both of your body language."

He sighed. "Yeah, you're right. Think we can go on another date sometime?"

Her face broke into its widest grin yet. "I'll commit to two, but nothing past that, so you better make those count." She leaned forward and stood on her toes to kiss his cheek. "I'll catch up with you in a while." She walked past him, and as he turned to watch her go, he saw why she'd left so suddenly.

Cia strode up and punched him in the arm, hard.

"Ow, damn. Jerk."

She laughed and clapped her hands. "You're the jerk. So, I hear that I'm stuck with you."

He scowled. "This place is like a cesspool of gossip. What the actual hell?"

"I corralled Stephenson when the beautiful Dr. Cray distracted you."

"Ah. That makes sense." He grinned. "Yeah, I'll be around. Think you could teach me to pilot the *Grace*?"

The pilot frowned. "That's a pretty big ask."

"What if I said please?"

She shook her head. "More."

He sighed. "Pretty please?"

"Now you're talking." She grinned. "I'm thinking of

doing a little work for the family. You can help me not kill them all in the process."

"Done deal."

She excused herself and ran to Ethan Kimmel. He shook his head. *They make a really cute couple.*

Athena replied, "I'll never admit to having said this, but you and Dr. Cray do as well."

He nodded. *I'm not sure what the future holds, but I'm glad that she and Cia, and you will be a part of it. Now, I have to tell my Special Forces team that I'm not coming back.*

Athena laughed. "So they can start celebrating, you mean? Sounds good, liven up the party. Also, we need to discuss getting me an android body to control. I mean, imagine the possibilities if there was one of me in your head and another at your side."

Jax shook his head and laughed as he headed off to rejoin the party, confident that whatever lay ahead, he'd be in fine company to meet it.

THE END

FEDERAL AGENTS OF MAGIC

Have you read Federal Agents of Magic from TR Cameron and Michael Anderle? Book One is Magic Ops and it's available now from Amazon and through Kindle Unlimited.

FBI Agent Diana Sheen is an agent with a secret....

...she carries a badge and a troll, along with a little magic.

But her Most Wanted List is going to take a little extra effort.

She'll have to embrace her powers and up her game to take down new threats.

Not to mention deal with the troll that's adopted her.

All signs point to a serious threat lurking just beyond sight, pulling the strings to put the forces of good in harm's way.

Magic or mundane, you break the law, and Diana's gonna find you, tag you, and bring you in. Watch out magical baddies, this agent can level the playing field.

It's all in a day's work for the newest Federal Agent of Magic.

Get your copy today at Amazon or Kindle Unlimited

Get sneak peeks, exclusive giveaways, behind the scenes content, and more.
PLUS you'll be notified of special **one day only fan pricing** on new releases.

Sign up today to get free stories.

or visit: https://marthacarr.com/read-free-stories/

What a ride! This was a fun one to write, especially after the reversals Jax and his team faced in book 3. I hope you're satisfied with the ending. I especially enjoyed seeing how Athena grew and developed. I switched back to narration for this book, and was again reminded why I prefer to draft with my voice. I think the dialogue is snappier and the description thicker when I can get it all out faster. There's no real time savings in the long run, because editing takes longer, but I do like the results.

I'd love to write a spinoff buddy comedy with Jax, Athena, and Cia. I think it'd be hilarious. Won't happen anytime soon, though, because we're headed in a different direction – more on that below.

The anticipated battle for Nintendo Switch time manifested, resulting in a second Switch in the household. Naturally, as soon as we did that, the kid discovered that Fortnite is even more fun on a PC. But, you know, things go around. Eventually the Switch will be back in household vogue.

A while back we got an Oculus Quest to play Beat Saber, because Beat Saber is phenomenal fun. Then they made it possible to hook it up to a PC. So now, as soon as I can pry the kid away from their machine, I'm going to try out Half-Life: Alix. It's been a long time since my last Half-Life game, and I'm eager to fix that. I'm also eagerly awaiting Cyberpunk 2077.

So, passive entertainment wise, you must watch Amazon's *The Boys*. It's rude, crude, bloody, and phenomenal. Seriously. Also, a little show I love called *The Expanse* is coming back in December. I'm so very excited for that.

Those who follow me on Facebook know that we've added two more kittens to the house. Again, we wanted one. We picked two that didn't look much like each other out of the set of photos, and naturally, they were brothers. We couldn't split them up. So, two. They act more like baby goats than cats, hopping around and chasing each other all over the place. The others aren't so welcoming just yet. Lots of hissing. But they'll be in one-room quarantine for a while longer, so there's time.

The kid and I are watching movies in the car a few evenings a week. Kind of a homebrew drive in. My wife brings us snacks. It's proved to be more fun than I thought it would be when Dylan suggested it. I should have known better. So far, *Onward, Angry Birds,* and *Shark Boy and Lavagirl.* I was dubious about the last one until I discovered it was Robert Rodriguez, who I pretty much love.

So, next up is a trip back to the Oriceran Universe. I'm working with Martha Carr to build out a formerly secret race of elves, some new fantastical creatures, and a killer storyline. I'm really excited for this one. It'll be in the same part of the timeline I've been writing in, so there's some potential for familiar characters to show up from time to time.

Finally, if you enjoyed this book, you might like my other science fiction series, and maybe even my Urban Fantasy. It's all filled with action, snark, and villains who think they're heroes. The Sci-fi series in particular has some great spaceship combat stuff, a lot of politics and machinations, and some cool technology. Plus so much snarky banter, you can't even believe it. Drop by www. trcameron.com and take a look!

Until next time, Joys upon joys to you and yours – so may it be.

PS: If you'd like to chat with me, here's the place. I check in daily or more: https://www.facebook.com/ AuthorTRCameron. Often I put up interesting and/or silly content there, as well. For more info on my books, and to join my reader's group, please visit www.trcameron.com.

I recently had curtains made for the living room. Not exactly big news. But I realized once they were hung that this was the first time I had treated a home like I play to stay. Really stay.

This is not a house I bought, this is a home where I have roots.

Roots are not something I've always been particularly good at cultivating. I'm a late-blooming wanderer who doesn't travel lightly. I take everything I own with me.

Frankly, most of the time I've preferred to live as if I could get up and go at any time. The first time I bought a piece of furniture that would be really difficult to move I had to sit down and breathe deeply for a little bit. I felt trapped by that piece of furniture.

I'm not sure when that idea started with me. Probably when I was very small and constantly wishing to be rescued, which never happened. That is until I was forty-seven years old and finally found the courage to leave everything I knew and just go. I packed up a U-Haul with what I could, sold the rest and drove north humming the theme song to the Mary Tyler Moore show.

I was unleashed on the world and I've never looked back.

I'm not looking back now but I've also stopped looking forward to the next spot. It turns out that when it came to picking a spot there were a few requirements (it helps to find a place where you're one of many who are just like you and not the only one – tip for those of you still searching), but it also takes a conscious choice to say, this is where I'm staying.

Instead of the anticipation of the new, there's a richness that comes from getting to know the deeper layers of people and places. Sure, some people still move on and we lose touch and some places, particularly in 2020, disappear and are replaced. But knowing who or what was there before still adds to the experience. Plus, I've found it takes on average about two years to really just settle into a new place, and trust me this one I know. If I'm not doing that grand move anymore, there's no longer a steep learning curve. I can focus on other things instead. Learn a hobby, find cool places to hang out, hidden nooks of Austin, and really create a nest.

My new motto is I'm going to make this house so personal it will be an issue for the Offspring once I'm gone. First up, besides curtains, will be the gardens coming in the spring. The plans for them are awesome and HOA approved and of course pictures will be forthcoming in the fan group on Facebook. It will be my secret garden complete with singing cartoon birds and small rabbits (I kind of hope – the dogs may find that too interesting).

This new life plan is so radical for me that I wonder how it will affect other things. I'll let you know. More adventures to follow.

CONNECT WITH THE AUTHORS

TR Cameron Social

Website:
www.trcameron.com

Facebook:
https://www.facebook.com/AuthorTRCameron

Martha Carr Social

Website:
http://www.marthacarr.com

Facebook:
https://www.facebook.com/groups/MarthaCarrFans/

Michael Anderle Social

Michael Anderle Social
Website:
http://www.lmbpn.com

Email List:
http://lmbpn.com/email/

Facebook :
https://www.facebook.com/LMBPNPublishing